MOREAU SEMINARY LIBRARY
NOTRE DAME, INDIANA 46556

SINE QUA NUN

Other Books by
Monica Quill
AND THEN THERE WAS NUN
LET US PREY
NOT A BLESSED THING
NUN OF THE ABOVE

SINE QUA NUN

A
SISTER MARY TERESA
MYSTERY
BY

Monica Quill

THE VANGUARD PRESS
New York

PZ
4
Q54
Sin
1986

Copyright © 1986 by Monica Quill.
Published by Vanguard Press, Inc., 424 Madison Avenue, New York, N.Y. 10017.
Published simultaneously in Canada by Book Center, Inc., Montreal, Quebec.
All rights reserved.
No part of this publication may be reproduced or transmitted in any form or by
any means, electronic or mechanical, including photocopy, recording or any in-
formation or retrieval system, or otherwise, without the written permission of
the publisher, except by a reviewer who may wish to quote brief passages in connec-
tion with a review for a newspaper, magazine, radio, or television.
Designer: Tom Bevans
Manufactured in the United States of America

Library of Congress Cataloging-in-Publication Data

————————.
     Sine qua nun.

     I. Title.
PS3563.A31166S5 1986   813'.54   86-19107
ISBN 0-8149-0926-4

MOREAU
SEMINARY
LIBRARY

SEP 11 '86

for
Raoul and Sandy Kunert

One

The studios of WRZR would have been hard to find in decent weather, but today, with even the main streets clogged with snow and treacherously icy and side streets more like toboggan slides than thoroughfares, the short trip turned into an adventure.

Kim was at the wheel of the Volkswagen, Sister Mary Teresa was wedged into the passenger seat, her breath visible in impatient puffs though her profile was hidden by her headdress, and Joyce was in the back seat. It was Joyce who likened the side streets to toboggan slides. Kim would have preferred her to keep reading off the street signs.

"Riverdale," Emtee Dempsey exhaled. She might have been smoking.

"Two more should be Fremont," Joyce said. "You turn west."

"Right or left?"

"West is left," Emtee Dempsey said. She had the uncanny knack of always knowing precisely in what direction she was headed, nor had age dulled the accuracy of her inner gyroscope. Kim got around Chicago without reference to directions, but they were now in a part of the city unfamiliar to her.

"Why are they located way out here in the boondocks?" she asked. Her neck was sore from trying to peer through the steamy windshield.

Emtee Dempsey took her remark as a question rather than a complaint and gave a little lecture on the flight of television studios from the Loop into the western suburbs.

"Fremont," Joyce cried out. "Take a left."

The frozen ruts on Fremont had been made by cars with a wider wheelbase than the Volkswagen's and Kim slid from trough to trough, spinning the steering wheel to keep their progress generally forward. A tantalizing block ahead, beyond a cross street, was the entrance to the studio parking lot, just as it had been described by Rick Kettler when he gave directions.

"You can't miss it," the producer had assured Kim.

How right he was, and in a sense he had not intended. Approaching the final intersection, Kim applied the brakes. Nothing happened. Or rather what happened was a sense of speed that had nothing to do with the motor. The car slid into the intersection, accompanied by the irate horn of a delivery truck that had been lumbering south and now went into a half spin as the driver tried to brake. Kim caught a fleeting indelible glimpse of his face, a mixture of terror and wrath. But the Volkswagen skated safely by and into the parking lot, where a patch of shoveled and dry pavement arrested the car with a jolt.

Limp with fear, Kim turned to Emtee Dempsey, expecting a reaction to their brush with death, but none came. Nor did Joyce say anything about the narrowly avoided collision except that the driver had gone on. Did she think he could have stopped on that ice?

"Two minutes of eleven," Emtee Dempsey reported, having punched the stem of the watch she had extracted from a bosom pocket. She was due for the taping of the Basil Murphy Show at eleven and nothing could distract her from an appointment to be kept.

"Sorry I'm late," Kim said with an edge to her voice.

"I would not have wanted to be here a minute sooner," Emtee Dempsey said.

"You nearly weren't."

Why expect the old nun to react to an almost-collision with a truck? It had not been the only chancy moment in the drive, though it was certainly the worst, but Emtee Dempsey, having prevailed over Kim's suggestion that they call the studio and say the weather prevented keeping the appointment, had made up her mind to treat the trip as mere routine. On the other hand, she could have been concentrating on what she might be asked on the Murphy Show and hence ignore the terrors of the unfilmed world.

When Rick Kettler had telephoned and asked if Sister Mary Teresa Dempsey was still perhaps alive, Kim reacted with a laugh.

"I take that to mean she is?"

"Very much so."

"Forgive the directness of the question, but if the an-

swer were no, that would be it." Rick Kettler then identified himself as the producer of the Basil Murphy Show.
"Do you know it?"

"Yes."

A little pause. Had he expected a more enthusiastic
response? "Mr. Murphy thinks people are curious about
nuns and he wants to devote a half-hour segment to the
subject. We've lined up Faith Hope to represent the new
nun and Sister Mary Teresa was suggested as representa-
tive of a more traditional outlook."

"Suggested by whom?"

"Faith Hope. Do you think Sister Mary Teresa would
be interested? I assume she is quite old."

"Ancient. But very peppy. I'll put you through to her."

There was the sound of a throat being cleared. "I am
already on the line," said the voice of Emtee Dempsey.
"Tell me more about the show, young man."

"You've never seen it?"

"I was referring to the show about nuns. You needn't
stay on, Sister Kimberly."

Kim had taken the call in the kitchen and hung up the
phone decisively. Joyce noticed her pique and stopped
loading her food processor. "What?"

"The Basil Murphy Show."

"No kidding." Joyce was impressed. "Do they want
her on?"

"That's the idea."

"What topic?"

"Nuns."

"Good grief." Joyce made a face. "Do they think nuns
are still news?"

"I guess so. They need someone to balance Faith Hope. She suggested Emtee Dempsey."

"Well, maybe Faith Hope is news." But Joyce's regard for the Basil Murphy Show had obviously suffered a blow.

Faith Hope was news indeed. Hope was her family name and the superior who had selected her name in religion either had not thought of the combination—barely possible—or had an odd sense of humor. Nowadays most nuns had reverted to their baptismal names, but Faith Hope preferred the striking conjunction that had come her way on taking the veil. Whenever she made news she was invariably referred to as an activist or dissident. And she had dissented from much and been extremely active besides. Most recently she had been in the news because of her suggestion that nuns sever all connections with the Catholic Church so as to acquire full freedom of action. "As one might give up breathing to be less dependent on the biosphere," Emtee Dempsey had commented. Kim doubted that Sister Faith Hope could count on the charity of Sister Mary Teresa. However photogenic the dissident activist might be, she would be no dialectical match for the old nun.

The light on the kitchen phone told them the conversation with Rick Kettler was a long one. Would Emtee Dempsey accept or reject? Neither Kim nor Joyce had the least doubt. The old nun was unlikely to forgo an opportunity to make known her views on what some benighted souls chose to regard as progress.

She accepted, and a date was set for when the show would be broadcast live locally and filmed for syndication through the country. Three days before the appointed Friday, snow began to fall on Chicago. It came from the west, it came from the north, it came off the lake. Chicago was a blur of white. It was the worst snowfall of the season. It reminded commentators, who could not have been alive at the time, of the great snow of '88.

On Wednesday morning the radio was full of cancellation and closing announcements. The Kennedy, Eisenhower, and Stevenson expressways were slick and dangerous, with the result that public transportation reeled under the burden of new clients. Unnecessary trips were advised against. Eleven deaths were ascribed to the weather during the first forty-eight hours of the storm. By Thursday the city looked as it must have looked a century before under such weather conditions. Even in the Loop the few people about used the streets as walkways, hurrying between huge mounds of snow pushed to curbside. Then, on Friday, the snow stopped and the sun came out.

"I thought it would never end," Emtee Dempsey said with a sigh of relief.

"This may be only a pause. Anyway, the snow isn't going to just melt away. It's not twenty above."

"The storm is over," the old nun said. "This is an exact replica of the storm of 1937."

Emtee Dempsey had no doubt at all that the Basil Murphy Show would go on as scheduled.

"How do you plan to get to the studio?"

"We can't drive?"

"Have you looked outside?"

"Very well. We'll go by cab."

Kim glanced at Joyce. "I suppose we could try. I'll check to see if anyone is at the studio."

She phoned and Rick Kettler was not in yet, so she talked to his assistant. "I'm Lorrie. I was just going to call and check if Sister Mary Teresa will be here at eleven."

"Then the show hasn't been canceled." Kim had the feeling she was saying something faintly sacrilegious.

"I'm here. Rick's on his way. Mr. Murphy has not missed a show in seven years. We are counting on Sister Mary Teresa."

Kim felt chided. Maybe radio and television had exaggerated the difficulties of driving. Nonetheless, she suggested to Lorrie that it might not be wise to take a woman in her late seventies into the snowfilled streets unnecessarily. The girl was very upset. Kim decided to leave it up to the old nun.

"Of course I am going. I made an appointment and I intend to keep it."

No argument could have prevailed. The bright sunshine at the windows undermined anything Kim might say. She herself began to believe the storm was over.

And so they had set off, the three of them, in the battered little Volkswagen, on one of the most terrifying drives Kim had ever made. Now, at the main studio of WRZR, parked at the entrance as the old nun huffed and puffed, freeing herself from the seat and finally letting Kim pull her from the car, there was no admission that the drive had been anything but routine.

Joyce offered to park the car so Kim could accompany Sister Mary Teresa up the steps and into the studio. Salt had been strewn on the steps to melt the ice, but they looked dangerous nonetheless. Kim insisted that Emtee Dempsey lean on her arm and stop showing off.

"They know how old you are. You don't have to act like a novice."

"Nor like an invalid."

But she took Kim's arm and they mounted the steps one at a time and went through revolving doors into the welcome warmth. The appearance of the short chubby nun all done up in her habit, the enormous headdress quivering over her round face, caused a sensation. A receptionist who must spend her day greeting celebrities major and minor lost her aplomb entirely at the sight of Emtee Dempsey. A portly man seated in the lobby looked up from his open briefcase with rounded eyes, mouth agape. A boy hurrying through the lobby put on the brakes and stared. Kim, at the side of the object of all this attention, took satisfaction from the entrance Emtee Dempsey had effortlessly and perhaps unconsciously made.

The receptionist, fiftyish, red hair, green eye shadow, her decolletage more daring since she must look up at visitors, concentrated on Kim with eyes glistening behind their contacts.

"The Basil Murphy Show," Kim told her.

The woman nodded. A smile refused to form on her painted lips. Sneaking a look at Emtee Dempsey, she picked up a phone to announce their arrival. "Please be seated. Someone will come for you."

The someone was Lorrie, thin as a rail, her indecisively blonde hair worn in a sort of Orphan Annie style. She glowed when she saw Emtee Dempsey.

"Great! Perfect! I was hoping you'd wear something like that."

"That" was the habit of the Order of Martha and Mary.

"My dear, I have been wearing it for nearly sixty years."

"Wow!"

Kim introduced herself and Lorrie made a swift comparison. Kim wondered how badly she suffered from it even though Rick Kettler's assistant clearly regarded religious habits as theatrical costumes. "You look wonderful," Lorrie said to the old nun. "Mr. Murphy will be so pleased."

They waited for Joyce, then went with Lorrie to an elevator, descended one floor, and were taken to a small room in which there was a large round table, mirrors on three walls, and a monitor mounted in the corner.

"This is where guests wait until they're ready to go on."

"Guests? We are alone."

"Mr. Murphy is doing the first segment now." Lorrie pointed a nibbled nail at the monitor. "Geoffrey Chaser."

"You're not serious," Emtee Dempsey said.

"That's him in the corduroy coat."

"I meant the name." Emtee Dempsey's eyes were drawn to the screen, where an enormous man with wild gray hair, his opened shirt displaying several gold chains and wearing indeed a corduroy coat, was holding forth. Soundlessly. The audio on the monitor had been turned down. And then Basil Murphy appeared on the screen.

An oversized head set on diminutive shoulders, eyes flashing with intelligence and, at the moment, sardonic skepticism. His hands lifted and then dropped back on the arms of his wheelchair.

"Wanna hear?" Lorrie asked.

~ 9 ~

Joyce nodded and turned up the sound. Before the male voices filled the room, Emtee Dempsey repeated in wonderment, "Geoffrey Chaser."

"He's a writer," Joyce explained.

Emptee Dempsey groaned but attended to the screen. Basil Murphy was speaking.

"Then you don't really deny that your novels are based on real happenings and real people?"

"Any writer who denied that would be a liar."

"Your critics say you simply reconstruct what has happened—they emphasize 'simply'—rather than show what might have been."

"What has happened might happen," Chaser said, his even teeth appearing beneath his mustache in a smile.

"*Ab esse ad posse valet illatio,*" the old nun murmured.

The sheets of paper scattered on the table before them proved to be a brief vita of Geoffrey Chaser. Kim picked one up, glanced at it and passed it to Emtee Dempsey. The old nun, seeing what it was, put it into her purse. Of course. She was a pack rat, returning to the house from any excursion with handouts, fliers, newspapers. Anything readable and free exercised an irresistible fascination on the old nun.

They had come in at the midpoint of Murphy's interview with Geoffrey Chaser and this gave Sister Mary Teresa an opportunity to see the nature of the program. Basil Murphy was a gifted interviewer, whether with a single guest or several, managing to elicit not only information but also the latent character of his guests. He allowed them to reveal themselves, usually unwittingly, to his audience.

Unobtrusive and short-winded himself, he nonetheless was a constant presence throughout the half-hour segments. Kim swiftly gained the impression that she was learning far more about Geoffrey Chaser than she cared to know.

The name was a pen name, of course, adopted when its bearer made the transition from columnist for an obscure suburban paper to sensational novelist. His first effort, a paperback original, was called *Canterbury Tails* and would have gone the way of such soft porn if it had provided no more than the mandatory titillation of the reader. But his characters were somehow real, the action gripping even when not erotic, the writing accomplished. After several years as what is called, in the inflated jargon of the book trade, an underground classic, the novel was brought out in hardback by a major publisher, an unheard-of inversion of the usual process. Scholars would have noted a toning down of the prurient parts from the paperback version, but the story remained steamy enough to sell in enormous numbers. Geoffrey Chaser was a publishing phenomenon beyond the dreams of avarice.

Nor was he a one-book wonder. Titles poured from his word processor at annual intervals, one more successful than the last. They came to be called "romans à clay" because of their debunking effect. In one lurid novel a lady mayor of Chicago was thinly disguised. ("Thinly would be disguise indeed," Chaser chortled.) She had taken it well, observing that if she were half as bad as the heroine, her political career might not have come to so untimely an end. Other objects of Chaser's attention were not so philosophical. His current novel, *Gruel Treatment,* was commonly thought to be an attack on Madelaine Marr, who for three decades had run a shelter for the homeless in the Loop. Seen through the lens of Geoffrey Chaser's skeptical glasses, Madelaine—in the book she was Magdalene Carey—was an opportunist who amassed a fortune by banking the bulk of the contributions she received for her charitable work. The fictional philanthropist was a Messalina as well, enabling Chaser to—in his own words—keep hitting his reader below the belt.

"You don't need me to tell you who your heroine is taken to be modeled on," Basil Murphy was saying.

"She is a composite character."

"There are sources other than Madelaine Marr?"

It seemed melodramatic to think of Chaser's smile as evil, but Kim could think of no other description. He leered at the camera. He seemed to implicate the viewer in his sleazy activities. There was an odious animal cunning in his eyes.

"You don't expect me to accept the assumption of your question."

"Meaning that Madelaine Marr is not the basis for your character Magdalene Carey? The parallels are obvious. The center on State Street, her appearance..."

"My lawyer tells me that Madelaine Marr has nothing to do with Magdalene Carey." Spittle bubbled in the corners of Chaser's mouth as he grinned.

"I do not want to listen to any more of that man," Emtee Dempsey said emphatically. She had been put into a rotating chair and now spun away from the monitor. Joyce got up and turned it off. Lorrie seemed undecided what to make of this rejection of the Basil Murphy Show.

"Anyone want coffee?"

"Would you have some tea, my dear?"

"Where do you get it?" Joyce asked. "I'll help."

After Joyce and Lorrie left, Emtee Dempsey rotated 180 degrees. "Turn it on again. That man is impossible."

Kim knew what Sister Mary Teresa meant, and it was not entirely with reluctance that she turned on the monitor again. Like the old nun, she wanted to see more of the odious Geoffrey Chaser.

But the interview was finished and the square face of Basil Murphy filled the screen. He was thanking Geoffrey Chaser and opining that his viewers would have valued this chance to hear the controversial novelist defend himself.

"When we return, my guests will be two nuns. Faith Hope, who has been much in the news lately, and Sister Mary Teresa Dempsey, one of the grand old ladies of Chicago higher education, long-time professor of medieval history."

Fade. Lorrie hurried in with a paper cup in each hand. "Tea," she said, handing one to Emtee Dempsey and glancing at the monitor. "Yipes. The first segment is done. I'll be right back."

Lorrie fled with the other cup, but Joyce had brought coffee for herself and Kim.

"Where is Sister Faith Hope?" Emtee Dempsey wondered aloud.

"Maybe they keep guests waiting in different rooms."

"Or maybe the weather stopped her," Kim suggested.

"The weather?"

"Forget it."

Lorrie came back with a young man taller than she was. He wore a pullover, his hair looked as if he had just pulled it over, and eyes suggestive of an aquarium peered from very thick lenses with visible fingerprints all over the lenses.

"I'm Rick. Bad news. Well, news. Faith Hope won't be here. So we'll just go ahead without her, okay?"

"What happened to her?" Kim asked.

Emtee Dempsey said, "Of course I'll go on." She sounded like an old trouper. Joyce hummed a few bars of "There's No Business Like Show Business." Meanwhile, Rick was pulling Emtee Dempsey, chair and all, into the corridor. Kim objected.

"I think Sister would prefer to walk."

"Sorry," Rick said distractedly. "Habit." He got in front of them, clipboard in hand, running his long fingers through his hair. The sleeves of his sweater were pushed halfway up his arms, he wore tattered sneakers, he seemed a nervous wreck.

"Now, there's nothing to be worried about," he called over his shoulder. "Have you been on television before?"

"Young man, I was on radio."

"It's coming back."

"I will not wear make-up."

"No problem. We don't have time anyway."

"No make-up," Lorrie repeated. Now she seemed as jumpy as Rick.

"We wouldn't want to spoil your school-girl complexion," Kim teased.

They turned a corner and continued down another hall. Suddenly, coming toward them, was the unmistakable figure of Geoffrey Chaser, with Basil Murphy rolling along beside him. It was there in the hallway, after hurried introductions, that the host made his extraordinary proposal.

"Mr. Chaser is game, Sister. Are you? Admittedly, you make an unusual combination, but it could prove interesting."

The old nun took the extended hand of the novelist and looked closely at him as Murphy developed the suggestion that the two of them do the next half-hour segment together.

"And what would the theme be?"

"Have you read any of my novels?" Chaser asked her.

"Have you read any of my books?"

"What are they called?"

"By reviewers? Modesty forbids."

"I meant the titles."

"Oh, I doubt that you would recognize them."

"Don't be so sure. I have an M.A. in history."

"Do you really?"

"From Loyola."

"Are you Catholic?"

"I was."

Basil Murphy followed this exchange with interest. Off camera, he was less impressive than on, at least initially, merely a handicapped man in a wheelchair, his useless legs in clamps, his upper body keglike. But the force of his personality overcame the disadvantage of seeing the world from a seated position.

"Stop," he cried, holding up his hand. "Save it for the camera. Let's go."

He wheeled around and rolled swiftly toward the double doors of his studio, with Rick hurrying along beside him. Geoffrey Chaser turned his attention to Lorrie.

"I thought you'd stay for the show."

"Oh, I have lots of jobs."

"How did I do?"

"We can run the tape later if you like."

"Could I have it on cassette?"

He could have it on cassette. Kim went ahead with Emtee Dempsey, almost reluctant to leave Lorrie to the attentions of the leering Geoffrey Chaser.

The studio was dominated by three cameras, and the set was brightly illumined, leaving the corners of the studio in shadow. Rick hurried about settling people while Basil Murphy wheeled into place, ignoring his guests now as he studied notes Rick had given him. Kim made herself unobtrusive in an alcove behind one of the camera crews among sets for other shows: false kitchen cabinets, a real sink, what seemed to be a bar.

Basil Murphy sat at one end of a rectangular coffee table. To his right were two chairs of the same kind as those in the waiting room. Emtee Dempsey was put immediately to Murphy's right and Chaser was directed to the chair beside her.

The camera crews were getting Emtee Dempsey into focus, trying close-ups, making her chubby face fill the monitor screens. Television is a medium where participants are spectators. Guests and host could watch their own performances on the monitors positioned about the studio. The little old nun seemed indifferent to her visage looming at her from various points in the dark beyond the light-flooded set. Maybe she was blinded by the lights.

Unintelligible exchanges went on between Murphy and the camera crews. He seemed more in charge than Rick Kettler. A very large clock measured off the final seconds of the commercial break.

"Everyone ready?" He smiled at Emtee Dempsey and she nodded.

"Let 'em roll," Geoffrey Chaser said.

Music swelled and on the monitor a full shot of the set provided a backdrop for the running of the title of the show. And then Murphy addressed the camera.

"Welcome back to the Basil Murphy Show. Those of you watching us live have enjoyed a slightly longer than usual interval between segments, but I think you will agree the wait was worth it. My guest during the first part of today's program was Geoffrey Chaser. He has agreed to stay on in order to take part in an unexpected and of course unstructured discussion with Sister Mary Teresa. Sister Faith Hope was scheduled to appear but has been unable to be with us. Those of you watching in Chicago need not be told of the weather. Now you may well wonder what a medieval historian of Sister Mary Teresa's reputation makes of the novels of Geoffrey Chaser. Sister?"

"I certainly don't think much of the nom de plume. Chaucer is one of my very favorite medieval authors."

"Really? I'm shocked." Chaser's brows danced. "I am not half as ribald as Geoffrey Chaucer."

"I am sure there are many things you are not half as much of as Geoffrey Chaucer," Emtee Dempsey said sweetly. "To call him ribald bespeaks an adolescent mind."

"'The Miller's Tale'?"

"Delightfully comic."

"'The Nun's Priest's Tale'?"

"Taken all in all, *The Canterbury Tales* is one of the landmarks of European literature. To see in it only an occasion for schoolboy snickering seems beneath comment."

"Then let us move on," Murphy said, clearly happy with this beginning. "Do you read much contemporary fiction, Sister?"

"If you are asking if I have read any of Mr. Chaser's novels, the answer is No."

"I'll send you some," the author said.

"How many are there?"

"My ninth is on press."

"Ninth!"

"Trollope and Dickens were far more prolific, Sister."

Emtee Dempsey threw up her hands. "First Chaucer, now Trollope and Dickens. Have you no shame?"

"Not really. As a matter of fact, I enjoy irritating the kind of mind you represent. The fastidious, proprietary reader of nineteenth-century novels. I do indeed liken myself to Trollope and Dickens, and I don't mean that I am a dickens of a trollop. Their contemporaries felt toward them as you feel toward me."

The little nun turned her chair toward Chaser and the studio lights glittered from her glasses. "I do not mean to be unkind."

"You only want to call me a hack."

"Not even that, Mr. Chaser." She closed her eyes and shook her head. "What *is* your real name?"

It was Basil Murphy who answered. "Melvin Conroy. But I think we should continue to address him as Geoffrey Chaser."

"I will take that as a compliment."

Murphy said, "You were raised a Catholic, Geoffrey.

What do you think of the changes that have taken place in the Church in recent years? With particular reference to nuns?"

"I am appalled." He seemed to mean it. He turned to Emtee Dempsey. "The way you just sat down and began scolding me? I like that. That's the way I remember nuns. I'd prefer nuns to act as they do in Chaucer rather than run around in miniskirts and mascara, babbling about things they don't understand."

From her position behind Kettler, Kim was conscious of a glance from Lorrie. Although her skirt was of modest length, she wore no make-up and at the moment her lips were sealed. Kim wished she were sitting where Emtee Dempsey was.

"Now, Melvin," the old nun said, "don't confuse externals with internals. The origin of most religious garb is simply the fashion of a given day. The Vatican Council asked us to think of ways to be more effective in our work. A more simplified manner of dress was thought to be one way of doing that."

Kim could not believe her ears. This was the woman who had fought tooth and nail against changes in the Order of Martha and Mary, who had opposed the closing of the college and the selling off of the property, all proceeds going to the poor. Her warnings had been amply vindicated when nuns who had insisted on more relevant work and modern dress had gone over the wall in droves. The Order of Martha and Mary was now three nuns, a house on Walton Street that had been designed by Frank Lloyd Wright, and a lake home in Indiana.

"Yet you yourself wear the traditional garb of your order," Basil Murphy observed.

"We were given a choice. I find the habit more comfortable. And warmer in these Chicago winters."

"Do you know Madelaine Marr, Sister?"

"I do indeed. She is a genuinely great lady."

"If I had anticipated this confrontation between yourself and Geoffrey Chaser, I would have sent you a copy of his latest novel, *Gruel Treatment*."

Emtee Dempsey looked at the author. "You do have a way with words, don't you?"

Chaser smiled. "Actually, that was my second choice."

"What was the first?" the host inquired.

"I was afraid you wouldn't ask. *God's Swill*."

Even the camera crews groaned, much to Geoffrey Chaser's delight. Basil Murphy explained, for the benefit of Sister Mary Teresa, that the novel was generally thought to be a malicious caricature of Madelaine Marr.

"Will you write a novel about me?" Emtee Dempsey asked.

"I *am* at my most effective when I write about women. However, as between the two of you, Basil here might prove a better basis for my kind of fiction."

"How do you mean?" Murphy's smile seemed oddly fixed.

"Admittedly, a celebrity provides better inspiration when his career is on the upswing. Nonetheless, a deserved declension has dramatic possibilities of its own."

"Like Jane Byrne?"

"*I* thought she'd be re-elected. So did my publisher."

"That sounds like an admission that your novels are indeed veiled attacks on real people."

Chaser ignored this. From her position in the dark, Kim felt that a new tension had come onto the set. She could half believe it was for this that Basil Murphy had asked Geoffrey Chaser to stay on with Emtee Dempsey. There certainly was not much discussion of nuns.

"You have the added attraction of your handicap. People like you too often escape objective estimates of their performance. There is always the smallest taint of pity in the praise."

"And of contempt."

Emtee Dempsey leaned forward. "Do you intend to write a novel in which Mr. Murphy will figure?"

Chaser grew cautious. He crossed and uncrossed his legs and gave the old nun a big smile. "I have been accepting an assumption of our host, Sister. I do not say that I base my stories on real people in the manner suggested."

"Answer the question," Murphy said, his voice tense.

"It would have to be rephrased, Basil."

"Then rephrase it and answer it."

"And usurp your function? Really, Basil, you *are* losing your touch."

The redhead from the reception desk looked around the great piece of canvas that hung between the set and the hall door. She waved a slip of paper at Lorrie until the girl began picking her way delicately around the edges of the set toward her. Lorrie took the slip of paper and Kim watched her as she read it. Lorrie's reaction was theatrical, that of a schoolgirl. Her mouth popped open, then she clapped her hand over it and looked about her. A moment later, she pressed the slip of paper into Rick Kettler's hand.

The producer's reaction went swiftly from surprise to delight. He caught Murphy's eye and got the paper to the host of the show.

Murphy was annoyed by this interruption and for

some minutes ignored the paper while he bore in on Chaser, insisting that the novelist reveal the theme of his next novel.

"Are you putting in a bid, Basil?"

"Sooner or later you will run into a victim who refuses to be passive."

Emtee Dempsey intervened to say she thought a novel based on Murphy would be extremely interesting. "I looked you up, Mr. Murphy. You have had an extraordinary career."

"Past tense?" Chaser asked.

Murphy glared at the author, snatched up the paper, and glanced at it. His manner changed completely.

"Excuse me, Sister. I have just been handed a rather extraordinary message. I must assume it is not a hoax, although I have no way of knowing, one way or the other. But any supposition other than that it is genuine could jeopardize the life of the woman who should be with us on this set now."

He looked seriously into the camera for a moment, then lifted the slip of paper and read.

WE ARE HOLDING FAITH HOPE HOSTAGE.
GOD IS NOT MOCKED.
PRAY THAT HER LIFE MAY BE SPARED.
ISHMAEL.

Two

Into the startled silence that followed Basil Murphy's reading of the note the voice of Geoffrey Chaser entered.

"Of all the ridiculous nonsense. A threatening note to be read on a taped program? This is really the pits, Murphy."

Murphy gripped the arms of his chair and lifted his crippled body in a manifestation of strength. "This session is carried live, Chaser, to local viewers. The tape is for syndication and reruns."

"I think the announcement was for syndication." The soft-porn author shook his head in moral shock. "This is worthy of a cheap novel. The joke is it probably won't do a damned thing for your ratings."

"May I see the note?" Emtee Dempsey asked.

Murphy gave it to her. "It's a memo made by the receptionist who took the call."

"Ah," Chaser said. "Your accomplice."

Murphy picked up a glass of water from the table before him and dashed it into Chaser's face. The author rose, sputtering, on tiptoe as if belatedly to dance away from the watery contempt of Basil Murphy. Between the two men, Emtee Dempsey turned now to the one, now to the other, following the altercation with unperturbed fascination. Her expression suggested that nothing any man might do, be it ever so irrational, could strike her as unusual. But she was clearly on the qui vive for any escalation that might threaten her with a similar shower.

Geoffrey Chaser, his sardonic condescension gone, pushed past the old nun and bent to grab Basil Murphy's wrists. A fatal mistake. Like many handicapped men, Murphy had compensated for the loss of agility in his lower body by building up his upper to Herculean proportions. It was he who grabbed Geoffrey Chaser's wrists and, with a twisting motion, brought the author, his face contorted in pain, to his knees.

"I will accept your apology, Melvin Conroy."

"Apology!" But the word ended in a rising whine of pain.

"Gentlemen, gentlemen," Emtee Dempsey crooned, but Kim had the idea that the old nun was enjoying this. Kim could not repress a sense of satisfaction at the sight of the sarcastic author humbled before the camera. The camera! As far as Kim could tell, this whole episode was being caught by the hungry lenses of the onlooking television cameras.

"Let me go," Chaser said, squeezing the words out singly through gritted teeth.

Basil Murphy disdainfully pushed his kneeling guest away, spun his chair around, and wheeled rapidly from the set, with Rick Kettler hurrying after. As they left, the producer called over his shoulder, "Kill the cameras."

Lorrie got to Emtee Dempsey before Joyce and Kim did and pulled the chair vacated by Chaser close to the nun and sat in it. Almost immediately, she was on her feet again, looking down at the chair with distaste. "It's all wet."

"So am I," Geoffrey Chaser said, attempting to regain the manner that had been swept away when Basil Murphy threw water at him.

Lorrie, apparently deciding she could not get any wetter, sat down again and put a hand on Emtee Dempsey's arm. "Sister, I am so sorry."

"You're sorry? How do you think I feel?" Geoffrey Chaser's expression invited sympathy, laughter, some camaraderie, however grudging. But the four women only glanced at him, then ignored him. "I am going to get dry," he said.

"Yes," Joyce whispered. "Please do dry up."

"Are you all right, Sister?" Lorrie asked.

"I haven't had such an interesting afternoon in ages. Was all that actually televised?"

"Rick signaled to stop broadcasting when Mr. Murphy began to get into it with Geoffrey Chaser. It was recorded, though." She shook her head. "What a confusing program it was. It wasn't fair to you, Sister. Nothing went the way I planned."

"Have the police been informed about the phone call?"

"It was the first thing I thought of."

"Wise girl."

"I'll reschedule, Sister. We will have the program we planned."

"Better find out what happened to Sister Faith Hope first."

On the way back to Walton Street, the icy streets seemed tame after the contretemps—Sister Mary Teresa's word—at the studio. In the back seat, Joyce recalled what had happened, again and again, clearly unable to believe it.

"He actually attacked a cripple in a wheelchair. The fact that Murphy was stronger doesn't change that. What kind of man would attack a cripple?"

"A man like Geoffrey Chaser," Kim answered.

In the passenger seat, Emtee Dempsey hummed and smiled, dimpling her cheeks, happy as a lark.

"What in heaven's name happened to Faith Hope?" Kim asked.

"Oh, I wouldn't worry about her," Sister Mary Teresa said.

"Sister!"

"Even radical dissidents are human," Joyce added.

"You misunderstand me. I doubt that she is in any danger."

"How can you possibly know that?"

"I said I *doubted* one thing, not that I *know* something else. That which I doubt to be true I think to be untrue, but I do not *know* it to be untrue."

Joyce groaned. "Should I be taking notes?"

"A clear understanding of the logical relations among various propositions is not to be disdained, Sister Joyce."

Kim said, "Why do you think Faith Hope is all right?"

"Physically all right. Who do you suppose Ishmael is?"

"In the Bible?"

"Not in *Moby Dick*, my dear. I think—think, not know—that the note was a ruse."

"Phoned in by Faith Hope?"

The old nun looked unblinkingly at Kim. "That is your suggestion, Sister. Not mine."

It was not an hour later that the object of this discussion was seated in Emtee Dempsey's study, on the opposite side of the old nun's desk, mad—angry—as a hatter.

"Did you see the program?" Emtee Dempsey asked.

"Watch Basil Murphy? Please."

"But you agreed to appear on his show."

"I did not agree. I was contacted."

"You did not agree to appear on the Basil Murphy Show?"

"I discussed the matter in a preliminary way. Someone called. I expected a follow-up call, and when it didn't come I put it out of my mind. To tell you the truth, I was relieved. I have never forgiven Basil Murphy for what he put Sister Ophelia Yancey through when she agreed to appear on his program, badgering her about Mother Teresa, for heaven's sake. If I did not reject the feeler out of hand, it was with the idea that I might do a thing or two to make up for what that man did."

"Phoning in the threat could accomplish that."

"What do you mean?"

"Let me ask you outright, Sister. Did you telephone the studio and give that message to the receptionist?"

Faith Hope leaned forward, then sat back in her chair. Kim could see how angry the woman was. She wore a sacklike maroon dress that might have belonged to Katherine Senski. A string of beads the size of large marbles and as colorful hung around her neck. She had tucked in her chin as first reaction to Emtee Dempsey's question and now, sitting back, lifted it. This had the effect of drawing attention to her throat, not her most attractive feature. The lower part of Faith Hope's face sagged, giving the impression that she was melting with age. Bootlike shoes lent her a look of solidity, but the expression that formed on her face was of one unjustly accused, more sad than angry with her accuser, the look of a professional martyr. It was an article of Faith Hope's creed that she and all other women were the victims of male oppression. Perhaps she regarded Emtee Dempsey as an unwitting instrument of the oppressor.

"No."

Just no. She did not fume and profess indignation, she simply denied the implied accusation and Kim felt there was no possible way she could be doubted. Kim realized how disappointed Emtee Dempsey would have been if she had received an equivocal answer. Emtee Dempsey looked neither glad nor sad at Faith Hope's response, but there was little doubt that she believed it.

"The idea is absurd, but it seemed best to rid ourselves of the possibility at once."

"I wonder if you really think it absurd. What reason did you suppose I might have for doing such a thing?"

"It was something Geoffrey Chaser said about Basil Murphy."

"Geoffrey Chaser?"

"It's a long story."

"You don't mean the novelist?"

"You must watch the rerun of today's Basil Murphy Show. Mr. Chaser was your substitute."

Faith Hope found this delightful. "Have you read his books? They're marvelous. Not at all what their reputation would lead you to expect. He has genuine style and, in my view, a real gift for showing the flaws in human character."

"Have you ever met him?" Emtee Dempsey asked, her tone giving no special significance to the question.

"How I wish I had been on that program!"

"Well, of course, if you had been there, the two of us would have performed and I doubt we should ever have met Melvin Conroy."

Faith Hope frowned in incomprehension.

"That is his real name."

"Mel-vin Con-roy?"

Was she committing the name to memory? "Well, I already feel in his debt for the pleasure he has given me with his books. If he gave Basil Murphy a bad time, I say good for him."

"I find it odd that one with your ideological outlook would take the part of a pornographer."

"Pornographer? I wonder. Not that I'm against pornography," she added defiantly. "In any case, Chaser uses the genre ironically. It's really a big putdown of male chauvinism. His heroines always get the last laugh. Do you have any of his books here?"

"I don't believe so," Emtee Dempsey drawled. Her

eyes crossed ever so slightly when she turned to Kim to ask, "Do we, Sister?"

"No."

"Sister Joyce wouldn't have a copy or two lying about?"

"No, Sister."

Faith Hope did not seem to catch the playfulness of this exchange. "If Chaser gave Basil Murphy a bad time, I'm all for it. Murphy is the real chauvinist. That came out in the attack on Ophelia. Ophelia had asked him to admit how much his career depended on his wife. He attacked her savagely from that point on."

"His wife?"

Faith Hope bounced in her chair. "Good point! Of course, that was it! Ophelia was a target of opportunity because he could not face up to his hatred for his wife."

"Hatred?"

"All very subtle, as you had the intuition to see. Basil Murphy was excessively gallant to his wife, more concealed contempt. 'Let me seat you, my dear, Let me open that big heavy door for you.'" Faith Hope shook her head in disgust. "He would kill anyone who harmed his wife, as witness his attack on poor Ophelia. Yet Ophelia was a stand-in for the wife as well. You are a student of psychology, Sister Mary Teresa."

Emtee Dempsey permitted a smile to replace the frown on her chubby face. "I had been looking forward to discussing the religious life with you, Sister."

"That you will permit me to doubt."

"Permission denied. I did not say I looked forward to enjoying your views, let alone agreeing with them. But I think the public is owed a presentation of a more traditional, and orthodox, view of our life."

"I would have pushed my proposal that religious orders for women liberate themselves from a male-dominated Church and proceed on their own."

"Into oblivion? How many fewer members in your order are there today than a decade ago, Sister?"

Faith Hope huffed. "Why should women want to become nuns under the present regime?"

"Has it ever occurred to you that it is what you advocate that explains the dramatic decline in vocations?"

Faith Hope's mouth opened and closed. She paused to gain possession of herself. "Perhaps it is just as well we did not appear together, Sister Mary Teresa. I respect you. I admire you. I am quite sincere about that. You are without argument one of the most accomplished women in the Church. But you did it against the grain. However much recognition you have received, it has been given reluctantly. Men do not want to think us capable of anything truly important."

It was Emtee Dempsey's turn to gain control of herself. Kim could have formulated some of the old nun's responses to such remarks. Heaven knew she had heard them often enough. The old nun nodded.

"Sister," she said, "you should know that the assistant director of the Basil Murphy Show intends to reschedule us. I, of course, will agree to appear. I hope you will do the same."

"After my strange experience with them today, I don't know."

"You owe it to yourself to appear. Certainly Basil

Murphy owes you a chance to comment on the odd announcement he broadcast."

Faith Hope liked that line of thought. "We'll see."

"The young woman's name is Lorrie..." She turned to Kim. "What is her family name?"

"She didn't say. All she said was Lorrie."

Her name was Lorrie Rione and she called the house the following morning. "I have to talk to Sister Mary Teresa."

"Are you rescheduling so soon?"

To Kim's surprise, the girl burst into tears. Finally, through her sobs, she asked if she could come to the house immediately.

She wore a hooded coat of simulated fur, purple slacks pushed into knee-high boots, and sniffled while stamping snow from her feet for two minutes while Kim stood shivering in the open doorway.

"Did you see it?" she asked when she finally came inside and peered at Kim with bloodshot eyes.

"It" was a copy of the *Tribune* that she relinquished when Kim showed puzzlement. The story was in the second section, but there was no need to hunt for it. The paper was folded open to display it. Leering from the page was the unforgettable visage of Geoffrey Chaser under a headline: Talk Show Host Turns Hoaxer. Kim helped Lorrie off with her things and led her down the hall to Emtee Dempsey's study.

Even in her distress the girl could not disguise the impact the room made on her. Kim tried to see it with Lorrie's eyes, three walls of books from floor to ceiling, the fourth wall a window bracketed by more shelves. And Sister Mary Teresa, seated at the massive desk, as she was every day, doing her pages with an oversized fountain pen, the pile of manuscript at her elbow representing her long-term, final scholarly project, an intellectual history of the twelfth century.

"All these books," the girl said, turning slowly to take them in. "I wish Mr. Murphy could see this room."

"No reason why he cannot."

But Lorrie burst into tears as she had on the telephone. Kim put an arm around the girl and got her seated across from Emtee Dempsey. She had mentioned that Lorrie had cried on the phone, not something calculated to endear her to the old nun. That women were thought to be quicker to tears than men was, in Sister Mary Teresa's opinion, a myth. What was true, she conceded, was that women had the bad habit of using tears as a means to gaining sympathy when they did not deserve it. But even she was moved by the sight of the girl with the absurd hairdo weeping helplessly.

"What is it, my dear?"

Kim handed Emtee Dempsey the *Tribune*, giving her something to do while Lorrie composed herself. For a few moments there was only the sound of Lorrie's subsiding sniffling and the rustle of the newspaper.

"Mr. Geoffrey Chaser is even more malicious than I would have thought." She returned the paper to Kim.

In a special to the *Tribune*, Chaser gave his own very biased version of what had happened the day before, when the Basil Murphy Show went prematurely into commercials, breaking off a discussion that was clearly going full tilt. The accusations that had been more or less muted in the studio were openly made in the article. Basil Murphy was described as a setting star, once the centerpiece of Chicago television, his show syndicated for later showing around the nation, a magnet that drew celebrities of all sorts: Melvin Belli, Ralph Nader, Jesse Jackson, "stars of stage, screen, and radio." Kim wondered if Chaser or an editor had put the cliché in quotation marks. The article was unstinting in its build-up of the Basil Murphy who had been. That was needed for purposes of contrast. The show was now in steep decline. "A fact I had very much in mind when I consented, after much importuning, to appear. An author is always well advised to plug his books whenever and wherever he can and I was mindful, modesty allows me to say, that my appearance might do a thing or two to arrest the decline of Murphy's fortunes. For this admittedly mixed act of charity I was repaid with bodily attack in front of witnesses, and verbal abuse that will have been recorded on film as well as broadcast live to local viewers. My lawyer is presently seeking possession of a copy of the show." The burden of the piece was that a demented Murphy had engaged in an unprovoked attack on the novelist.

"And I've been fired," Lorrie sobbed.

"Fired! Why?"

"I told Mr. Murphy the note was my idea and he was furious. I don't really blame him."

"The note about Faith Hope?"

Lorrie nodded. "It was a stupid idea. I can see that now. I should have talked it over with Rick. But it seemed an inspiration at the time."

"Was Sister Faith Hope asked to appear on the show?"

"I contacted her and she dodged, asking me to call back. That's when I got the idea. Geoffrey Chaser was my idea too, but Rick knew of that and saw right away it was, well, a stroke of genius. Mr. Murphy was worried sick about the novel Chaser was supposedly writing and this would give him a chance to expose Chaser before he attacked Mr. Murphy. Now things are infinitely worse. I *deserve* to be fired."

Lorrie went into a second phase, self-accusation, self-contempt, her own worst enemy. She had no idea why Basil had hired her in the first place. "Oh, I do too. It was because of my cousin Remy, his lawyer. I couldn't even get a job without that kind of help."

Emtee Dempsey had Joyce make hot chocolate, insisting on cookies as well—there were freshly baked ginger snaps she could not wait to taste—and gradually calmed Lorrie down, establishing an atmosphere of sisterly companionship. Joyce joined them, and together they got the inside story of the Basil Murphy Show.

Basil Stephen Murphy—known as BS to irreverent friends—had been born in Galesburg, Illinois, attended Notre Dame, became a writer for the fledgling WRZR shortly after receiving his degree in Communication Arts under the tutelage of the renowned Professor Thomas Stritch. It seemed a suitable job for a man who had been one of the last victims of polio and was destined to live his life in a wheelchair. But if others might think of Murphy in terms of subsidiary roles, he himself yearned for the top. And he got there by excelling in everything he did. The punctiliousness of his scripts became legend: no need to worry about any misstated facts or unverified claims in anything Murphy wrote. What no one had imagined was his effectiveness on camera, something that came to light one winter day when Murphy was almost alone to make it to the studio during a snowstorm. ("Another snowstorm," Emtee Dempsey murmured. "He should have recognized the portent.") For more than five hours he kept WRZR on the air almost singlehanded, and viewers, bound to their sets by the weather, phoned in record numbers to express their appreciation.

Things were never quite the same again for Basil Murphy. One of the admirers he gained that day was Nancy Shale, an enormously wealthy woman five years his senior, widow thanks to the much-publicized disappearance of her husband, Henry Shale, from his boat in Lake Michigan. The sloop Henry had prided himself on being able to sail crewless was found crewless indeed, and without Henry either, riding the waves of the lake seven hours after Henry had left Mackinack. Nancy had brought money to the marriage and took a good deal more from it after Henry was declared legally dead. Whether more than Basil Murphy's talent, intelligence, and drive to excel entered into the passion she formed for him, only her psychiatrist knew for sure. In any case, the improbable couple soon seemed as natural a conjunction as any pair of male and female, and few were surprised when eventually Nancy wheeled Basil down the aisle, his beaming wife in a stunning soft blue outfit enhancing the sheen in her prematurely gray hair that she preferred to emphasize boldly rather than rinse back into a semblance of youthfulness. Doubtless it was Nancy's directness, *savoir-vivre*, and devotion to himself that turned Basil's head. His handicap had led him to think of himself as condemned to celibacy, so his initial reaction to Nancy's overtures was wary. If there had been any objective advantage for her in showing such interest in him, his skepticism would have nipped their romance in the bud. Eventually the time came when Basil was able to accept the seemingly incredible fact that Nancy loved him. That what he felt for her could count as love seemed clear enough. What it could not count as was gratitude. Basil Murphy had steeled himself against reacting to common courtesy as if it were a heroic concession to his disability and thus was unlikely to respond to Nancy as to a benefactor.

The publicly unasked question was whether or not the marriage had been consummated. Or was consummatable. But of course it was whispered everywhere, by friend and foe alike. It would have been impossible to put such a question to Basil Murphy himself, needless to say, and not even Nancy's sister Sheilah could bring herself to formulate it in sisterly privacy, although she obliquely and persistently pursued the matter for some years after the marriage. This interest was eventually deflected by her own more flamboyant marriage to Austin Gregorovius, that most uxorious of theatrical impresarios whose third wife— or was it fourth? his stormy liaison with a tango artist in Buenos Aires was a dubious entry in the official record— she became. With Gregorovius, consummation was not only devoutly to be wished but all too regularly achieved, in and out of the appropriate matrimonial bed. Gregorovius had been the alleged basis of Geoffrey Chaser's third "roman à clay."

But back to Nancy and Basil. For five years, whatever conjugal secrets they did or did not have, theirs seemed an idyllic union. Nancy added to her whirlwind social life, into which Basil was swiftly wheeled, her role as his seven-day-a-week Girl Friday. It was not unjust to say it was as much due to her persistent promotion as to Basil Murphy's undoubted talent that the Basil Murphy Show—his getting his own show did, however, antedate their marriage—enjoyed the meteoric rise it did. Nancy was forever on the phone to possible guests and usually got the ones she and Basil most wanted. The net was soon flung far beyond Chicago. Within three years it could be called a genuinely national show. It achieved this status, not by means of a standard network, but by syndicating the tape of the show that was shown locally live.

The Basil Murphy Show brought a cosmopolitan flair to Chicago and nostalgic memories of the golden years when network shows had originated in the Windy City. Shades of Dave Garroway. On the set, during the show, Nancy was invisible, but throughout the week she ran interference for Basil. It was she whose insistence got him the distinctive décor forever afterward associated with the show and imitated by so many others. The officials of WRZR gritted their teeth and suffered Nancy's relentless championing of her husband because the results were inarguable. Basil Murphy was the hottest thing going in Chicago television. And so it was to be for a decade.

Pathologists of popularity might disagree as to exactly when the apogee was reached and the Basil Murphy Show, despite valiant and even frenzied efforts to retain what had been gained if further expansion was impossible, began undeniably to slip. The star quality of the guests dimmed slightly and here and there, like first leaves turning in autumn, stations failed to renew their contracts.

There were other more public elements in Basil Murphy's decline. The first was one of those peccadillos to which the wealthy are subject and that are seldom excused by their economic inferiors. A tax shelter into which Basil had been led by his own desire, the advice of Nancy, and the urging of his lawyer came under IRS investigation. The publicity was maximal; Basil and the other celebrities who were involved were made to look like swindlers, when they did not appear dupes of the Hungarian immigrant who had talked them out of their money on the basis of a prospectus for Brazilian silver mines.

And then there was the break-up with Nancy, precipitated by the attentions paid her by Pablo Quince, a rock star ten years her junior, whose agility on stage and, it was alleged, in more private performances, made for a striking contrast with the wheelchairbound Basil. It was this contrast, such is the cruelty of lovers when love has gone, that got into the explanations forced from Nancy by the press. She spoke of the difficulties of remaining in love with a mind alone. She, alas, was both body and soul. This was taken to be sufficient answer to the old question concerning consummation.

Without Nancy's constant overseeing, the Basil Murphy Show was not what it had been. Rick Kettler was brilliant, but the alterations he introduced to stanch the flow of vital fluids had small effect. By the time Sister Mary Teresa was invited onto the show, it was in steep and undeniable decline.

Kim glanced at Emtee Dempsey to see if this morose observation by Lorrie Rione disturbed the old nun's serene sense of who and what she was before God and man, but of course there was no reaction suggestive of petty vanity. Emtee Dempsey was clearly fascinated by the story of Basil Murphy and would soon set Kim the task of filling in the blanks from alternative sources. The fact that Basil Murphy himself had shown panic at the prospect of a novelization of his decline and fall by Geoffrey Chaser seemed to confirm that the end of his career was in sight.

Joyce said, "Such a novel might be just what the show needs."

"I told him that! I don't know how many guests have used the old line with me. 'Just spell my name right.' There's a lot to it. Who knows why people like what they like anyway? Basil wants to believe that all his viewers love him. But look at the Indianapolis 500."

"What do you mean, my dear?"

"It's pretty generally agreed that people watch auto races half hoping for a crash. And think of boxing matches."

"I will leave those to Sister Joyce," Emtee Dempsey said, and Joyce did a little comic shadow boxing in response. Joyce watched Top Rank Boxing every Thursday on ESPN.

"People want a knockout. But try to tell Basil that a good portion of his viewers have been waiting for him to get gored. He can't face the fact that he could hold on to them if he was willing to play the wounded gladiator."

"Young lady, you are a philosopher."

"I better be, now that I've lost my job."

"What exactly happened?"

"When I told him I arranged for that note, he hit the ceiling. With him, that consists of lifting himself off his chair by using the arms as parallel bars. Gored or not, he is as strong as a bull."

"I saw that yesterday. Why did you tell him you were responsible for the note?"

"Because he accused Rick of doing it." And she blushed. Kim wondered if there was anyone whose face so swiftly betrayed its owner as did Lorrie Rione's. What a sensitive girl she was, running the gamut of emotions as she spoke to Sister Mary Teresa. She had entered weeping, and while she spoke of Basil she had grown more and more dramatic. One might have thought she was half in love with her boss if the telltale blush and the fact that she had sacrificed herself to protect Rick Kettler had not shown the true direction of her affections.

"Murphy knew nothing about it?"

"No."

"But he knew you had talked to Faith Hope?"

"Oh, sure."

"And he thought she had agreed to come?"

The steel wool hairdo bobbed. "This was my idea." Lorrie sat forward as if she were selling her idea there and then. "First, a knockout segment with Geoffrey Chaser, in which Basil establishes his moral and intellectual authority over that sleazy man. A cluster of commercials to rinse the viewer's mind, and then Basil alone with you. A profound, knowledgeable exchange on the lamentable state of the Church today, maybe an oblique reference to the fact that Basil, abandoned by his wife, is still bound to her by the Sacrament of Matrimony, and all the while you are holding forth and it is clear that you think Basil Murphy is really okay and vice versa. Then the note! Think of it."

"I am."

"It had everything. When Basil decided to keep Geoffrey on for your segment, I thought, great. Then the contrast I wanted to establish between the segments would be even more obvious." Lorrie sat back. "I still think it was a great idea."

"It was."

"Thank you."

"I shall myself tell Basil Murphy he is a fool if he lets you go," Emtee Dempsey said. "The future of his show depends upon his recognizing your undeniable gifts."

"Oh, Rick will save Basil Murphy."

"Without your help?"

Again the blush. How old was Lorrie anyway? The mention of Rick could turn the show business whiz into a schoolgirl. But leave it to Emtee Dempsey.

"How old are you, Lorrie?"

"Thirty-one."

"A native of Chicago?"

"Rockford. I came here to attend DePaul and have been here ever since."

"All that time?" Emtee Dempsey murmured. "Well, young lady, what you did may help Basil Murphy, whatever he thinks, but in the meantime you have caused him a lot of trouble. That story." She gestured toward the newspaper. "Not that I think Melvin Conroy will sue. People who threaten to sue seldom do." She smiled. "I must make a gift of that couplet to Mr. Rush, our lawyer. But the story is bad enough. On first reading. Of course it tells a good deal more about its author than it does about its ostensible target. And it will tell against him more when people see that it was he who attacked a disabled man and was beaten for his pains. I myself might become the source of such information if the tape is not clear on that point. Faith Hope may be another story."

"You think she will sue?"

"Worse. I think she will demand to appear on the show and that you had better agree."

"Me? I've been fired."

"Tush. I'll take care of that."

She picked up the phone with a grand gesture, pressed it against her headdress where an ear would be, and looked blankly at the dial. Her eyes moved to Kim.

"Sister, would you ring WRZR for me and ask for Basil Murphy?"

"The number is 232-2960," Lorrie said.

"Good," Emtee Dempsey said, displaying a palm to Kim, who returned to her chair. Without need for repetition, she dialed the number. Kim wondered how long it had been since Emtee Dempsey herself had put through a call when there was someone in the room to do it for her.

There was some delay before Emtee Dempsey asked if she were speaking to the lovely woman with red hair who welcomed guests to the studio. Her tone was one of shameless flattery, but within moments she was speaking with Rick Kettler.

"What is this nonsense about Lorrie Rione?" She listened for a moment, a stern expression on her oval face, and then broke in. "I had best speak to Basil Murphy, Rick. Put me through to him. No? Well, give me his home number then." Emtee Dempsey glanced toward the gesturing Lorrie. "No, that's all right. Just leave a note saying I called."

Lorrie had Basil Murphy's unlisted number and this time Sister Mary Teresa permitted Kim to put through the call. Or at least to attempt to. The phone rang and rang without being answered. Kim put it down, stopping the exchange between Lorrie and Emtee Dempsey. "No answer."

"Make a note of that number, Sister. We can try again later. When did you speak with Basil Murphy?" she asked Lorrie.

"He was in his office earlier. He could be at his club. The athletic club."

"I think I could have guessed that. No need to bother him there. How does he get around town?"

"He drives. His car is specially equipped so that everything is manual. Even the pedals."

Lorrie's smile was her most attractive feature. It was impossible to come within range of it and not have the impression that the girl was really beautiful. How lucky the Basil Murphys are to find assistants as dedicated as Lorrie. And then to fire her! Kim tried the number again, not wanting to postpone longer than was necessary Emtee Dempsey's talk with Basil Murphy. Kim had no doubt the talk-show host would crumble under the onslaught of the old nun's persuasive cajoling. But there was still no answer at Basil Murphy's apartment.

"Then try Katherine Senski." Emtee Dempsey tapped the folded paper with her index finger. "I would like to hear an explanation of how such a screed as this appeared in any paper Katherine Senski is associated with."

Katherine began to speak as soon as Kim identified herself. "Did he come? Sister, there was little I could do to stop him and I did not give him the address. After all, he can find it in the telephone directory. I did tell him that much, as a way of washing my hands of the whole matter, but surely even he would have thought of it sooner or later. Anyway, if she was willing to appear on television with that man before God knows how many million viewers, she has no complaint at all and I don't care what he told her."

"Are you talking about Geoffrey Chaser?"

Emtee Dempsey reached imperiously for the telephone and Kim relinquished it.

"Katherine, what is going on?"

She listened, a little smile coming and going on her lips, her eyes darting from Lorrie to Kim.

"I understand, Katherine. I understand. Katherine, we all make mistakes."

But her tone suggested there was one significant exception to that generalization who was too modest to mention her name.

"Katherine, I forgive you. Stop by this evening. Good. Five-thirty? So late? Very well. Come when you can."

After Lorrie left, the interlude before Katherine would come that evening seemed ready to be filled by Geoffrey Chaser.

Three

But Geoffrey Chaser had not put in an appearance at Walton Street before Katherine herself arrived, her heavy dark green cloak whipping in the winter wind as she came from cab to door like some half-foundering galleon seeking harbor. She gathered in the cloak as if to slow her progress, mounted the steps, and came right through the door Kim held open without any pretense of getting the snow from her shoes. Boots, rather. Cowboy boots.

"Katherine, what on earth are you wearing?" Kim pointed at the older woman's footwear.

"They are ideal in this kind of weather. I bought them as a lark in Phoenix last year and tried them out when this storm started. I have half a mind to write an article advising their general wear in Chicago. Has he come?"

"Not yet."

"Thank God."

With something of a matador's flair, Katherine whipped off her cape and thundered down the hall to the study. The sound of boot heels brought Joyce to the door of her kitchen.

"What is she wearing?"

"Cowboy boots."

"She sounds like a runaway herd." But there was a look of naked envy in Joyce's eyes. Kim, wrestling Katherine's cape onto a hanger, wondered if the reporter would indeed start a fashion trend in snowbound Chicago. Katherine had been accomplishing the improbable all her life, the only sad note being that she had never married. But there had been a tragic love, a doomed passion to which she had devoted her life, a virgin, though not for the kingdom of heaven's sake. It was the one topic on which Katherine could not be quizzed, so of course it seemed to Kim and Joyce the most fascinating aspect of her story. So what if she had been the first lady of Chicago journalism since her early thirties? So what if she had been a trustee of the college and had fought its sale at Emtee Dempsey's side, their failure to prevent selling off the college binding the two old women more firmly than any success could have done? So what if she had written three books, miles of newspaper copy, and numbered two Pulitzers among her trophies? Katherine Senski had had a love that could not lead respectably anywhere and had accepted her fate, remained a friend to the man whose heart she could not claim, and acquired the tantalizing note of mystery.

When Kim came into the study Emtee Dempsey was

speaking. "Katherine, either he comes or he does not. The man is pitiable and my vocation prevents me from turning him away. Is he really as odious as he seems?"

"He is as odious as he is. Are you going to offer me a drink?"

"I will do better. I will give you one."

She actually picked up the phone and buzzed the kitchen. All by herself, without help. Lorrie's visit had had at least this happy effect. Emtee Dempsey asked Joyce to bring something for Katherine to drink. Sherry? Sherry was fine with Katherine.

"Sister Joyce, can you set another plate?"

Katherine began to protest, then thought better of it. Surely staying here with friends and enjoying one of Joyce's culinary triumphs was preferable to going back out into the snow.

Kim and Joyce often kidded about the two old women in their absence, but were more than fascinated by them. It was no hardship, therefore, to sit all but silently through the exchange between Sister Mary Teresa and Katherine Senski that began in the study and continued into the dining room, where Joyce's saltimbocca alla Romana added its delicious piquancy to the feast of conversation. Who would have thought a threatened visit by Geoffrey Chaser could be the occasion for so delightful an evening?

Katherine put Melvin Conroy, a.k.a. Geoffrey Chaser, before their eyes with professional deftness, providing a background for the man they had met in the studios of WRZR.

He lived quite near them, as it happened, which was why Katherine had been certain the author would have al-

ready made good on his resolve to come talk Sister Mary
Teresa into joining his crusade against Basil Murphy. A
small sound of disdainful dissent escaped from Emtee
Dempsey's pursed lips.

"How near?" she asked.

"Water Tower Place. And that, if you can believe it, is
little more than a pied-à-terre. He has a magnificent lake
place, not far from your own, now that I think of it, in Indiana on the shore of Lake Michigan. Vulgar display, you
will say, but it has been said before. What, after all, is Melvin Conroy's life and work if not vulgar display?"

This rhetorical question was followed by an account
that made it clear Katherine Senski had done her home-
work on Chicago's celebrated soft-porn novelist. Conroy
had been a fair to middling journalist, she said, who had
made much of the fact that he had turned down jobs at the
Tribune several times, both before and after his notoriety.
His column, of which he now spoke as if it had been an
achievement, had not, according to Katherine, been much
noticed prior to the appearance of his first novel, and he
had dropped it within a year of literary success—if that
was the right term.

"What kind of column was it?"

"In its way, it suggested the kind of book he would
write. He caught on, to the degree that he did, by attacking
people. This might have been dangerous, from a legal
point of view, if he had initiated the attack. But libel was
not much of a problem when the target of abuse was already in trouble—arrested, accused, whatever. Conroy
showed a real knack for jumping on people already down.
But it was his style that was very much his own."

Emtee Dempsey raised her brows quizzically.

"He could damn while at the same time exhibit cynicism about the standards of damnation. And he was witty, in a heavy-handed sort of way."

The old nun shook her head. "Wit, intelligence, apparently some gift for language. What a shame he has turned all that in the direction he has. Clearly it has coarsened him personally, beyond redemption from a human point of view. A fallen angel."

Katherine laughed. "Sister, you must be the only one in Chicago who ever called Melvin Conroy an angel, fallen or otherwise."

"*Corruptio optimi pessima.*"

"Please. Not while I'm eating. You know how terrible I am at foreign languages."

"Latin is not a foreign language."

"Tell it to the Greeks."

The appearance of Conroy-Chaser's first novel had, Katherine observed mordantly, brought out the worst in his journalistic colleagues, many of whom harbored the dream of writing a book and making a name outside the evanescent columns of a newspaper. That someone should actually have done this was like a judgment on those who had not, and for it to be so unprepossessing an individual as Melvin Conroy—well, this was more than the envious could bear. There was no need to guess who lay behind the silly pseudonym, of course; Conroy publicized the matter himself.

"Then why a pen name?"

"He may genuinely prefer to be called Geoffrey Chaser rather than Melvin Conroy."

"Sounds like a tie to me," Joyce said.

"Katherine, everything you have said about this man would explain why the *Tribune* should not have published his attack on Basil Murphy. Why did it?"

Katherine looked sadly at Emtee Dempsey, shaking her head. "Things are not as they were, Sister Mary Teresa. Standards have changed. Perhaps it would be truer to say that standards have all but ceased to exist. The young seem incapable of recognizing sensationalism as a problem. The great thing is competition. It was felt, and not without reason, that Chaser's piece would sell newspapers. And so, despite this weather, it did."

The old nun smiled. "I would be able to feel more righteous if I had not read it so avidly myself."

"It could be said, Sister, that you lost your right to complain about the *Tribune* when you teamed up with that man on television."

Emtee Dempsey laughed, as if she rather liked the suggestion she was a rogue. "Even so, you will give Basil Murphy the right to reply, will you not?"

"If I made such decisions, there would have been nothing to reply to, not in my newspaper."

Katherine's cab had scarcely pulled away from the curb in front of the house on Walton Street when another car pulled into the vacated space and Kim's brother hopped out. Richard clambered over the bank of snow, waving to catch Kim's attention. As if it would have been possible not to notice him, running around in this weather wearing only a suit. Nonetheless, Kim was tempted to ignore Richard, if only because his appearance at their doorstep usually spelled trouble.

"Richard, where is your overcoat?"

He seemed surprised he wasn't wearing it, then gestured toward the car. Inside the house, he shivered when the contrast between heat and cold struck him. Richard's red hair matched Kim's own and the look in his eye might have been her own—if she were trying to contain anger.

"Kim, one question and please just answer yes or no. Is Basil Murphy here?"

"Basil Murphy? Are you serious?"

He closed his eyes for a moment. "Yes or no. Which is it?"

"Do you have some reason to think he's here?"

Richard said, not quite aloud, a word seldom heard in this house and set off down the hallway toward the study. Before he reached the door, Emtee Dempsey appeared in it.

"Richard! I thought I heard your voice."

Richard seemed to think she meant to block his way. He sidled past her and looked around the study, an expectant expression dying on his face. He looked down at the old nun, trying to recapture his irate mood.

"You're looking for someone, Richard?"

"As if you didn't know."

"Well, I would certainly guess it. If you are looking for Katherine Senski, she just this moment left."

"I know."

The old nun joined her hands over her cane and looked up at him over the tops of her glasses. "I will not play guessing games."

"We are looking for Basil Murphy."

"Why?"

"Has he contacted you?"

"Why should he?"

"Look, can we sit? Obviously this is going to take a while."

They could sit, but in the living room, not the study. Richard's presumption in inspecting the study made it impossible for Sister Mary Teresa to welcome him there. He accepted the offer of a beer, got settled in a brocade chair, and rubbed his eyes.

"There was a note on Basil Murphy's desk saying you had tried to reach him."

"So that's it."

"Did he return your call?"

"What did Mr. Murphy tell you?"

"We can't find him."

"Why should you want to?"

He thought for a moment, then seemed to decide there was no point in holding back.

"The guy who calls himself Geoffrey Chaser has turned up dead."

"Dear God in heaven!"

"Dead. Killed. Strangled, with something other than hands. A garroting."

"Sister Joyce, put on water for tea," Sister Mary Teresa said, preparing for a long session and never mind the hour. "Tell me about it, Richard."

Geoffrey Chaser, né Melvin Conroy, had been found dead in the sitting room of the suite he kept in an exclusive residential hotel in the shadow of the Water Tower complex. Entrance to the hotel was controlled by a hostess seated at a desk within fifteen feet of the revolving doors. Before getting to her, a stranger would have had to negotiate two forbidding doormen. If the caller accomplished the impossible and managed to get by both doormen and the hostess, he had only three choices.

"He?" Emtee Dempsey asked.

"He or she. The murderer."

Was it possible to get used to that word? Kim wondered. Listening to Richard, remembering the detestable Conroy and the dislike she had felt for him from the first moment she saw him, Kim felt awful. Even while they had talked about him with Katherine the man would have been already dead. And not simply dead. Murdered. She had a vivid image of Basil Murphy grabbing the author's wrists and twisting him cruelly to his knees. No wonder Richard wanted to talk to Basil Murphy. Particularly after Chaser's savage attack on the talk-show host in the *Tribune*. But Richard's account of the difficulty of getting into the hotel made it improbable in the extreme that the handicapped Basil Murphy could have entered the Claremont without being noticed.

The three choices an intruder had were (a) to take a seat in the lobby, a diminutive area in Richard's description of it, no point of which was out of range of the hostess's eyes; (b) enter the little bar directly ahead where the one man who functioned as bartender and waiter joined the team of potential witnesses; and (c) to take the elevator to Conroy's suite, which added one of two elevator operators to the pool of potential witnesses.

"There are no stairs?"

"There are stairs. Call that the fourth possibility."

Emtee Dempsey bowed slightly, as if she had made an important point, but she was careful not to injure Richard's pride. There was still much she wanted him to tell her.

The only sign of a struggle was a coffee table pushed at an angle in the sitting room of the suite. The word processor at which he wrote seemed in order and it could be said that the notorious author had gone gently to meet his maker. But it soon became clear to the police that the apartment, particularly what had been called in a recent article Conroy's workspace, had been thoroughly rifled.

"The instrument of strangulation was not at the scene?"

Richard shook his head. "The place is being gone over in the usual way. Something should turn up. In the meantime, I want to talk to Basil Murphy."

"Why?"

Richard poured more beer into his glass, sipped it, put it down. "Tell me about your appearance on the Basil Murphy Show."

"Did you see it?"

"I intend to look at a tape."

"But you did hear of it?"

"I can read," Richard said ironically. "What did Katherine Senski want?"

"Richard Moriarity, you have the soul of a policeman. Does it ever occur to you that people do most of the things they do without anything like what would count as a reason in your sense?"

"Conroy's attack on Murphy appeared in her paper."

"That's right."

There seemed nowhere to go from there.

After a moment of silence, Emtee Dempsey said, "I hope you aren't done telling me about poor Melvin Conroy. Who found the body?"

"The elevator operator."

"Oh?"

"He was sent up to see if Conroy's phone was off the hook. It was."

"Knocked off the hook?"

"Maybe by Conroy himself."

The body had been found at five that afternoon. The edition of the *Tribune* in which Conroy's article on Basil Murphy appeared had come out at noon. Basil Murphy had been at his office throughout the morning, but he had not been seen since midday.

"Where did he have lunch?"

"He had a reservation at the Pump Room. He didn't show up."

"Did he intend to lunch alone?"

Richard shrugged off the question as diversionary.

"Have you looked for his car?"

"It is in the garage of the building in which he lives."

"Richard, why this desire to see Basil Murphy? The way you describe the murder scene, he is the last person in the world who could have eluded all those watchdogs, made it upstairs undetected, strangled that pitiable man, and then disappeared without being seen. You do know he's confined to a wheelchair? For him to show up at the door of that hotel would be a memorable event."

Richard frowned. "Because he was in Conway's room." He held up his hand to stop the old nun's protest. "So I didn't tell you everything. He was there. The imprint of his wheelchair was on the carpet. It's been checked with similar trackings in his office at WRZR. There's no doubt about it."

Emtee Dempsey fell silent, a silence more thoughtful than surprised. Kim wondered if she was thinking of the crippled man's rage and strength when he manhandled Melvin Conroy in the studio. The subsequent attack in the *Tribune* could only have increased that rage. How must the handicapped host have reacted to Conroy's selective account of what had gone on then? Knowing, thanks to Lorrie Rione, what they now did of Basil Murphy's troubles, it seemed plausible that as the cumulative effect of a long run of bad luck he had turned once more in anger on his most recent oppressor. In order to stop the novel supposedly based on his life? At the moment, that might have seemed like a mere bonus of the deed. The main thing would have been to strike back, to take arms against a sea of troubles and, by strangling, end them.

Kim was glad Emtee Dempsey could not tune into her somewhat baroque version of events. A version that made no sense. Given that Basil Murphy had indeed killed Conroy, given that he had had more than enough motivation, how could he possibly have gotten his chair to Conway's suite, killed him, and gotten away again?

Emtee Dempsey emerged from pensive silence. "Very well. Who are your other suspects?"

Richard laughed, looking to Kim for an accomplice, but she remained unsmilingly true to Emtee Dempsey. Not that she thought the question as silly as Richard did.

"Don't you believe me, Sister?"

"Richard Moriarity, one of the pillars of our relation-

~ 57 ~

ship is that I always unhesitatingly believe what you tell me."

"I wish I could say the same."

"Oh? Do you talk to yourself? Richard, I am serious. Who else do you think might have killed Melvin Conroy?"

"Besides yourself?"

"Besides myself." She had not blinked.

"Sister, Basil Murphy left his mark in Conroy's apartment. He was there. I wouldn't want to send the prosecutor to court with that alone, but it puts him at the scene of the crime beyond any doubt."

"But was he there at the time the crime was committed?"

"You think he was there at some other time?"

"You have shown that it was impossible for him to have been there today. Therefore I assume the mark of the wheel must have been made on the carpet at some earlier time. Like those in his office with which you must have compared it. No doubt one or more of those people you mentioned at the hotel will be able to tell you of that visit."

Kim turned away so that she did not have to see her brother's expression. Clearly he could not say that any of the hotel staff had mentioned an earlier visit.

"The important thing right now is that I want to talk to Basil Murphy."

"You do well to worry about him. I hope he has not suffered the same fate as Melvin Conroy."

Richard refused another beer, a decision Kim would normally have approved but tonight she wished her brother would stay until his self-esteem was restored. Emtee Dempsey obviously felt the same way.

"I know you or your colleagues will have spoken with the personnel at WRZR. Rick Kettler, as you know, told me Basil Murphy was not in when I called there earlier today. At the time, I thought that was very likely a mental reservation meaning that he was not in to me. But the fact that you found the note on his desk informing him of my call seems to remove that interpretation. Was the note written in Kettler's hand?"

Richard took a billfold from the inner pocket of his suit jacket and passed the note to Emtee Dempsey. "It had Basil Murphy's prints on it."

The old nun took the piece of paper and brought it close to the tip of her nose in order to squint skeptically at it.

"My name is misspelled. D-e-m-p-s-y." She handed the paper to Kim. "What do you think, Sister?"

"I never saw either man's handwriting."

"No more did I. I suppose you had samples for comparison there on Murphy's desk?"

"It's not written in Murphy's hand."

"And Rick Kettler said he had put it there?"

"No. He said you had telephoned and that Basil Murphy had not been in."

"Lorrie Rione was here this morning. She had just been fired by Basil Murphy. Naturally she was quite upset. We had a nice long talk and she gave us a good picture of how things have been going for Basil Murphy."

"Someone has talked with her."

"Of course."

"Maybe I will have another beer."

* * *

~ 59 ~

The following morning, after they had returned from Mass at the cathedral, always their place of worship when no priest was available to say Mass for them in the lovely little chapel in the house on Walton Street, Emtee Dempsey settled down with coffee, raisin toast, and all the papers, pouring over the accounts of the death of Melvin Conroy.

It is a truth generally recognized that newspaper people will accord one of their own attention far beyond any public claim—notices of the death of an Idaho editor, hitherto unheard of, for example, will be carried in all the Chicago papers. On that principle alone there would have been no surprise in the attention paid to Melvin Conroy's exit from this vale of tears. But this was not the usual send-off for a member of the fraternity. A note of malice, the suggestion that sometimes justice is visibly done, the inescapable sense that Conway had been universally hated by his fellow journalists, and, alas, the scent of envy, fairly lifted from the pages to which Emtee Dempsey devoted so much time, letting the twelfth century look after itself for the nonce. This was a more pressing matter.

Pressing, because she herself was concerned. Her name, the fact that she had appeared with Conroy on the Basil Murphy Show, figured prominently in all accounts. One paper had even had the audacity to say that neither Basil Murphy nor Sister Mary Teresa could be reached for comment.

"They do not claim to have tried," she admitted.

Finally she pushed the papers away, sat back, and looked fixedly ahead with a little smile bowing her lips. There followed the old nun's recital.

Melvin Conroy, who, under the improbable name of Geoffrey Chaser, had produced a string of semi-pornographic novels whose common note was that they amounted to thinly disguised exposés of easily recognizable victims, had been strangled in the sitting room of his suite in the Claremont Hotel, a block from Water Tower Place. No one had been observed going to or from the room and it would have been all but impossible to do so unobserved. Nonetheless, Melvin Conroy was dead, strangled after an apparent struggle. None of the papers, Emtee Dempsey noted, made mention of the mark of Basil Murphy's wheelchair.

"The police won't have to eat those words anyway," Kim observed.

"Oh, there is little doubt that Basil Murphy's chair was in the room."

"Do you think he did it?"

"I assume that Richard and his colleagues are completely satisfied it could not have been suicide."

"Melvin Conroy did not seem to be a man who would do any harm to himself."

"No? Look at what he had done to his own good name."

"Not in his eyes. He was obviously proud of his accomplishments."

"He did convey that impression. Assuming the mark of Murphy's chair was made some time prior to the murder removes the need to explain how he got up and down the stairs or elevator yesterday. But that calls for another ghostly murderer. The simplest solution to an impossible problem is to deny the existence of the problem. Rather than divert attention to the quest for a mysterious murderer who can pass unseen among so many people, it is tempting to say no such person exists. But Melvin Conroy is dead in his room, strangled. If he killed himself, no problem remains."

"That is pure speculation."

"Of course it is." Emtee Dempsey spoke with a certain pride.

When the phone on the desk began to ring, the old nun just looked at it, as if unsure what the instrument was for. How spoiled she was. Kim picked up the receiver.

"The Order of Martha and Mary," she said briskly.

There was no answering voice.

"Hello?" Kim said.

"Who's speaking?"

It was the unmistakable voice of Basil Murphy. Kim had not the least doubt of it. She passed the phone quickly to Sister Mary Teresa, forming in a silent exaggerated way the name of the caller.

"Mr. Murphy," Emtee Dempsey said, taking the phone. "I've been waiting for your call. I suggest that you come here. As you know, the house faces Walton Street. However, if you can get into the alley unseen, say from the street behind us, there is a back door through which you may enter."

The radiant expression on the old nun's face suggested that this opening salvo had the desired effect. But as she listened, her smile was replaced by a frown of concern.

"I see. Well, no matter. Sister Kimberly Moriarity will come fetch you. Accompanied by Sister Joyce," she added, lest anyone gain the impression that the three remaining members of the order founded by the Blessed Abigail Keineswegs were any less concerned than the foundress about giving scandal. "Our car is a disreputable Volkswagen." She pulled a watch from her bosom pocket and pressed its stem. It popped open and she said, "It is just 10:30 by my watch." She spoke as if this were equivalent to Greenwich mean time. "Where is the motel? On Lake Shore Drive. Sister should be there in..." Her brows lifted as she waited for Kim's estimate.

"Half an hour."

"They will be there at eleven. Do you have your chair with you? Ah. Very well. I shall be expecting you."

And so it was that in the gray midmorning of a January day in Chicago Kim and Joyce directed the little Volkswagen south along Lake Shore Drive to the motel where Basil Murphy awaited them. They could drive right to the door of his unit. He would be using crutches, not his chair.

"Crutches?" Kim had repeated.

But Emtee Dempsey had not wanted to pursue it. She picked up her fountain pen and unscrewed its cap. Kim was dismissed. While she and Joyce were gone the old nun would put in her daily stint on the massive intellectual history of the twelfth century she was writing. That easily she could switch mental gears, ridding her mind entirely of all the details she had derived from newspaper accounts of Melvin Conroy's death, repressing any excitement she felt at the prospect of discussing it with Basil Murphy. The matter was now in Kim's hands and, besides the main task of getting the television host to the house on Walton Street, she had to do this in such a way that his arrival went unobserved.

"Richard is not without suspicion," the old nun observed.

It was a moment when the call of blood was stronger than loyalty to her religious family, and Kim was tempted to inform Richard that Basil Murphy had contacted Sister Mary Teresa. But she pushed the thought aside. If he were being thorough, he could tap their phone. A highly inadvisable move, needless to say, since if Emtee Dempsey ever so much as suspected that Richard did not trust her—despite the fact that she regularly deceived him—there would be most uncomfortable consequences for the lieutenant of detectives, no matter that he was Sister Kimberly's brother.

Four

The sun had come out just enough to put a new glaze of ice on the streets and Kim once more felt at the helm of a luge as she directed the Volkswagen southward with Joyce beside her smoking a cigarette. She had to sneak them in the house, but here it did not matter.

"This is stale," Joyce said, rolling down the window and pitching out the cigarette. "Not very surprising either. It takes me weeks to get through a package."

"You should quit."

"First I'd have to start."

Joyce as co-pilot was superfluous, but Emtee Dempsey was a stickler for protocol—unless it served her purpose to waive the traveling-companion rule when she had pressing errands for Kim to run.

Recently Kim had read an article by a woman who had traveled cross-country by car alone and the tale was one of adventure and danger. The article lamented the fact that women still cannot avail themselves of the freedom of movement men take for granted without being subject to all kinds of mild and serious harassment. Kim had the idea that one is approached, by and large, because one is approachable. As a nun, she had taken the three traditional vows—poverty, chastity, and obedience. Poverty meant she made do with very little, stifled her acquisitive sense, did not permit things to gain power over her. But it certainly did not mean a life of deprivation. Obedience? That was another name for her relation to Sister Mary Teresa, who served as superior of their little community. Emtee Dempsey could be annoying, but Kim had such admiration for the old nun that she seldom needed to remind herself that docility to Emtee Dempsey was her way of exhibiting acceptance of God's will. And then there was chastity.

Kim had had crushes as a girl, but from the moment she entered the novitiate she had ceased to think of marriage or of any serious personal relationship with men. This had the effect of freeing her, enabling her to act with easy directness with both men and women. This was even truer of Sister Mary Teresa, but then, she had been at it much longer. The first effect of the vow of chastity is the disappearance of coquetry. Kim realized by contrast that hitherto there had always been the slightest element of flirtation in her contacts with men. The Bride of Christ. That was the traditional description of the nun. She has given her heart to Christ and this enables her to deal with others, men and women, with a simplicity and guilelessness that precluded the kinds of problems the author of the article mentioned. Not that Kim would wish to go on record saying the woman had crossed the country making goo-goo eyes at men and then complained at the response.

Basil Murphy awaited them in a motel located on a curve in the road in an area that had suffered when traffic was diverted onto the Skyway and expressways. Which gave some idea of the vintage of the place. Stuccoed, wood-trimmed, a sloping shingled roof, the place was in an advanced state of disrepair. The Hi Hat. A topper tipped in seedy insouciance on the weatherworn sign in front, the neon tubing that had framed it hanging loose. Kim would have preferred to see the sign at night—if it did indeed light up. What on earth was Basil Murphy doing in a dump like this?

The driveway had not been shoveled, but a sufficient amount of traffic in and out had kept it open and Kim slid in from the street, turned the wheel, and, for an eerie moment, continued straight ahead. Then the wheels caught and the car crept along the row of units the doors of which opened onto the snow-clogged parking lot. Murphy was in unit 13. Had that been a deliberate choice? Motels apparently did not cater to the superstitions of clients as hotels do. No car was parked before unit 13. A fresh dusting of snow made it unclear whether it was even occupied. But as Kim drew to a stop, there was a movement of the drape and then the door opened and Basil Murphy, propped on crutches, peered out, apparently blinded by the snow.

If he found this gloomy day bright, what a dungeon the motel unit must be! And indeed, there was no evidence of a light inside. Basil Murphy swung with surprising ease toward the car as Joyce hopped out to get into the back seat so he could maneuver into the passenger seat.

Murphy put one hand on top of the open door, the other on top of the car, somehow keeping the crutches under his arms, and looked carefully at Kim.

"Yes, I remember you." He put his head inside and looked at Joyce.

"I was at the studio too," Joyce said, sounding fearful that he might order her from the car.

"I don't remember."

"I'm sort of invisible."

"I wish I was."

He freed the crutches and handed them to Joyce, then swung around, backed into the seat, and reached down to lift his legs inside. He slammed the door so hard that snow slid from the car roof down the windshield, but Murphy had turned to stare at the motel, his breath steaming the window.

"What a dive."

"Don't you have any luggage?"

He grunted. "It's not my kind of motel. But it served my purposes. I wish I could go home and shower before seeing Sister Mary Teresa."

There seemed no reason to respond. Kim got the car in gear and let it creep on idle to the exit. Out of the way and bypassed by progress the motel might be, but the road going past it, old U.S. 12, still had enough traffic to make caution advisable.

The road up and the road down is the same road. Heraclitus. Then why did it seem twice the distance driving Basil Murphy to the house on Walton Street than it had getting to the motel? One reason was Kim's consciousness of Murphy's intense silence as they drove. At first she thought he was apprehensive because of the driving conditions, but that did not seem to be it. Nor did he respond to any overtures, whether from herself or from Joyce.

"It's supposed to snow more," Kim said.

Silence.

"Why are they always repairing roads in Chicago?" Joyce asked.

A shrug, but still silence.

How inane small talk is when it does not work. That kind of speech is not meant to make sense; it performs another function, like shaking hands, smiling, getting someone seated. Basil Murphy was clearly not in the mood for chatting and Kim was happy just to get him to Walton Street, where Emtee Dempsey could deal with the taciturn cripple.

As per instructions, Kim came along the street parallel to Walton that shared an alleyway with their house. She did not think much of this strategy, reasoning that if the house was being watched, Richard surely would have warned his men about the back door. The alternate entrance had once before, at least momentarily, fooled him. One thing about Richard, he could never be fooled twice in the same way. Luckily, Emtee Dempsey was ingenious in coming up with new ways. But the back door was a repeat and it would serve her right if it did not work.

Unless she did not intend to deceive the police.

Kim was once again impressed by Basil Murphy's agility with crutches. He swung with acrobatic ease up the steps and through the door into Joyce's kitchen where, resting his back against the refrigerator, he unzipped the suede jacket he was wearing. Belatedly it occurred to Kim that his clothing, like the Hi Hat Motel, was a kind of disguise. "What I would like more than anything in the world is a cup of coffee. The vending machine at the motel piddled discolored water that tasted like cardboard."

"Coming up," Joyce said, happy to get some kind of footing with the moody Murphy, who was looking around the room.

"What an interesting house."

"It was designed by Frank Lloyd Wright," Emtee Dempsey said in the doorway, surprising them all. But she had come down the hall without her cane. Perhaps out of consideration for Murphy's disability she did not want to draw attention to the fact that a cane made walking easier for her, though it was far from necessary. Murphy got to her in one swing of his crutches and put out his hand.

"Thank you for seeing me in this odd way, but odd things have been happening."

"Indeed. Come. I will show you the house." And off they went, down the hall, Emtee Dempsey calling back, "Sister Kimberly, you can bring coffee to us in the study when it is ready."

The house was still the topic when Kim brought the tray into the study. Basil Murphy was at ease in the chair across the desk from Emtee Dempsey and seemed quite knowledgeable about the Wright-designed homes in the area.

"I did not know of this one," he said.

"We do not want it included on tours."

"Quite right. It is a house, not a museum."

Murphy looked up at Kim when she gave him his coffee. "Please don't think I know anything of architecture. The hazard of the talk-show host is that he picks up a smattering of a thousand things but doesn't know anything well."

"So you have been hiding out in a motel," Emtee Dempsey said, marking the end of the first phase of Murphy's visit.

"And what a motel. As Sister here can tell you. It is what the police refer to as a hot-sheet place. A fast turnover."

Was the remark a test, to find out how shockable the old nun was?

"You felt you would be less likely to be found there?"

"I will take that as a compliment." He sipped his coffee a second time and returned the cup to its saucer. "You saw the account of the episode in the studio that Geoffrey Chaser published in the *Tribune?*"

"Yes."

"What do you think?"

"There is a saying that history is the victor's account of events. Not true, of course. As often as not, it is the loser's way of getting even."

Murphy said, "He's been murdered."

"Yes."

"That is not why I took refuge in the motel. If the TV account is correct, I was in the Hi Hat Motel when the murder was committed. Not that I would particularly care to use it for an alibi."

"Why where you there?"

"Because my life had been threatened." He had

picked up his cup and, having directed this dramatic remark over its rim, brought it to his lips, studying Emtee Dempsey as he finished his coffee.

"Obviously you took the threat seriously."

"It was Chaser. Conroy. He was still seething because of the way I humiliated him in the studio, and writing those lies for the *Tribune* had not satisfied him. He told me he would get me. When I least expected it. But that it would be soon. Yes, I took him seriously. I always take threats seriously. Always. My show is such that I run the risk of enraging weirdos. Threats are not uncommon. Attempts are rarer, but those too have occurred. I take it to be the part of prudence simply to get out of the way until the police have matters under control."

"You reported this threat to the police?"

"Of course. I have made use of the Hi Hat before. When I was young, it was quite different. A good restaurant, entertainment. I think of it as a kind of safe house."

"The police made no mention of Conroy's threat on your life."

"Well, it's a moot point now."

Emtee Dempsey shook her head slowly. "No. I am sure it would have been mentioned. You understand that they think you are responsible for Melvin Conroy's death."

"Nonsense."

"No, not nonsense. The accusation has at least prima facie plausibility. After all, he had written a novel about you."

"Not quite."

"You mean he hadn't finished?"

"No. It would have hurt me, but I was not the target."

~ 72 ~

"Have you seen it?"

"No comment."

"Hmm. Well, apart from any novel he had written, he had taunted you publicly on your own program. Men have killed for a good deal less than that."

"Don't misunderstand me. I do not have it in me to feel sorry Conroy is dead. The world will be a better place without him."

"That is not for us to say."

"I am simply being honest. He was a blight on the landscape."

"Why did you fire Lorrie Rione?"

He was genuinely surprised. "How did you know that?"

"She came to me. We talked. I think you have done her an injustice."

"I don't agree. She had placed me in danger of a libel suit. The note I read on the air? Pure fiction. Lorrie had concocted it herself."

"So she told me. And you know her motive. She was trying to help you."

He drew himself up, or at least half of himself, and tilted his chin. "If I were in need of help, I doubt that Lorrie would be the one to give it."

"Now, you know that isn't true. I will grant that Conroy was cruel in describing your present circumstances, but can you say he was wholly inaccurate? Things have not been going well with you, have they?"

"Show business has its ups and downs. Everybody knows that."

"Yes. And Lorrie knew it. She hit upon a device that,

given the standards of the entertainment world, was not completely out of line. But whatever she did, she did to boost your ratings."

"Tell it to my lawyer."

"Who is your lawyer?"

"Do you really want to know?"

"He is a cousin of Lorrie's, is he not?"

Murphy gave her a half smile that dimpled one cheek. "You've found out a lot of things, haven't you?"

"Oh, yes. About your wife, about your investments, quite a bit. It makes, as I said, a disturbing picture. It is one thing for you to resent Conroy's gloating account, but to fire Lorrie when she had nothing but your good in mind, well..."

"It was with my lawyer's knowledge that I was hiding out at the Hi Hat."

"So that, if we phoned and invited him here, no new element would be added?"

"Invite him here? What for?"

"Because, Mr. Murphy, you are in grievous danger, and I suspect your lawyer will see it more quickly than you. Meanwhile, you can hide here."

He laughed, a merry, full-throated laugh. "You would give refuge to a fugitive?"

"I would consider it an almost religious obligation to do so."

"But what if I'm guilty?"

"The right of sanctuary is not reserved for the innocent, Mr. Murphy."

If he had reacted to the offer as to a joke, within minutes he was more than interested, following Kim's description of the basement apartment with undisguised fascination.

"Hidden in a convent? It sounds like one of Geoffrey Chaser's plots."

"Shall we call your lawyer?"

"I get one phone call before settling in?"

"I am afraid there is no telephone in the basement apartment. Isn't that right, Sister?"

She was right. It had been removed when it had enabled a previous guest to communicate with the outside world without Emtee Dempsey's knowledge. As a rule, the basement apartment was offered to people the old nun wanted to keep an eye on. And, as well, to give her the exhilarating certainty that she knew things the police, meaning Richard, did not. The trump card of such knowledge could all too often be decisive.

Remy Carrero was very tall, with the dark skin of a Latin, thick hair brushed close to his beautifully shaped head, a touch of gray here and there, an aquiline nose down which he sighted at Kim.

"I am looking for Sister Mary Teresa." His tone suggested that he was fully prepared to share her amusement if he had come to the wrong door. Had he expected a convent building and been confused by the look of the house?

"Please come in. Sister is expecting you."

He wore a camel's hair coat, a silk paisley scarf, and gloves, which he peeled from his long hands with a surgeon's deftness. And waited. Clearly he was leaving the initiative to her, a lawyer's trick. Kim led him silently down the hall to the study. Within, alone, Emtee Dempsey sat at her desk, writing diligently. Her brows lifted, but her eyes remained focused on the page before her.

"Mr. Carrero."

"Come in, come in." Waving to the chair with one hand, finishing a sentence with the other, Emtee Dempsey could play a few games of her own.

"Please remain, Sister Kimberly. Well." She folded her hands and looked directly at her visitor. "Your client is in more trouble than he cares to admit."

"Would you begin by repeating what you said to me on the phone?"

"That I know where Basil Murphy is? Consider it repeated. But then, we both know where he is, don't we?"

"Where is Basil?"

"I was referring to the Hi Hat Motel. Mr. Carrero, if you are going to fence with me, we will get nowhere."

"He isn't at the motel."

"Not now. I arranged a transfer."

"To where?"

"Here."

Carrero looked around as if somehow Basil Murphy was in the study and he had not noticed him. "In this house?"

"That is correct. He will join us in a few minutes. Before he does, I want to put one question to you. Why were the police not told Basil Murphy's life had been threatened?"

He looked at her for a moment. He was an impossibly handsome man, a fact obviously not lost on himself. But he soon realized that charm of the usual sort would do him no good here. If he had been surprised to encounter a nun clothed in the flamboyant habit of the Order he had given no hint of it.

"Had Basil been threatened?"

"Mr. Carrero..."

"The question is genuine. I did not know Basil's life had been threatened."

"I see. Yet you knew he had taken a room at the Hi Hat Motel?"

"I wondered if he was there. He has gone there in the past. But it is impossible to get information from the desk, nor is it a place I should care to visit."

"Oh? Sister Kimberly drove there and brought Basil Murphy to this house."

"Did he telephone you?"

"Yes." Emtee Dempsey did not show the confusion at Carrero's answers that Kim felt. She sent the conversation in another direction. "Mr. Murphy does not take seriously the fact that police want to question him about the death of Melvin Conroy."

"Geoffrey Chaser. I don't blame Basil. It is ridiculous, apart from everything else, to think Basil could kill anyone. But the circumstances make it clear it was physically impossible for him to have killed Conroy."

"Why so?"

"Surely you have read the newspaper accounts."

Emtee Dempsey nodded.

"And you are aware of Basil's handicap?"

"You mean he would have been noticed?"

"Precisely."

"He was."

Whether this was a permissible use of the mark of the

wheelchair's tire, Kim could not say. But she knew that if Emtee Dempsey were queried about it, she would easily provide a plausible argument why it was not a lie. Carrero, in any case, was taken aback.

"He was seen at the Claremont Hotel?"

Emtee Dempsey's nod might have strained even her own theory. She said, "He is known to have been there."

"That was not in the papers."

"I have spoken with the police."

"You have?" Carrero became visibly cautious. He had let down his lawyer's guard but now it was up again. "How did that come about?"

"They came to see me."

Carrero thought about that. "To ask about the episode at the studio?"

"I was given a good many more details about the death of Melvin Conroy than appeared in the newspaper. I assure you that the police are very anxious to speak with your client."

"Have you informed them that Basil contacted you?" Carrero looked decidedly unhappy that he had accepted the invitation to come talk with Sister Mary Teresa. The interview was obviously not what he had expected and he seemed unsure how to proceed, or if to proceed. Suddenly he got to his feet. "If you haven't, I advise you to do so immediately." He might have been speaking for the record.

"In my interest or in that of your client?"

"I speak as an officer of the court. I am a lawyer, Sister Mary Teresa, and could hardly tell you anything else."

"And you have told me. Now, please be seated again."

Kim could not help thinking that it would be good if

Basil Murphy could listen in on his lawyer. Carrero seemed a man unlikely to let considerations of loyalty endanger him. How had Basil Murphy come to be associated with him?

"I have, of course, met your niece, Mr. Carrero. Lorrie Rione."

He nodded ever so slightly. Would he have denied the kinship if that proved prudent? Kim was sure he would.

"She has been fired."

"Sister Mary Teresa, you seem to keep yourself informed on a good many matters. I only wish I had the time and interest to discuss them with you. Could you call in Basil now? I assume he is the reason for this summons."

"Summons?" A lifting of the eyebrows. "As I remember, all that was necessary to get you here was to mention Basil Murphy's whereabouts. You invited yourself."

"Is Basil here?"

"Would you ask our guest if he'd like to speak with Mr. Carrero, Sister Kimberly?"

The old nun's tone suggested that she would advise against it. Was she regretful she had contacted the lawyer? But Basil Murphy must trust the man. Maybe Emtee Dempsey would find a way to tell Murphy he would be well advised to get another lawyer.

Basil Murphy had pulled a chair up to the television set in the sitting room of the basement apartment and was following attentively the program being aired. A busman's holiday? It turned out to be his own program.

"On tape. An old one. But good, I think. Do you know the senator?"

Kim knew the televised guest was a senator. "You must have had many programs to choose from to rerun."

"I didn't make the choice. It must have been Kettler. I am remaining incognito."

"Mr. Carrero is here."

"Good!" He put his hands on the arms of the chair and levered himself to his feet. Kim would have given him his crutches, but he impatiently waved off her attempt to help. Obviously, he had long ago made up his mind to be as little dependent on others as his handicap would allow. Kim stood aside and followed his surprisingly swift progress up the stairs to the study. When they passed the kitchen, Joyce looked up in surprise. Was she thinking, as Kim was, that the assumption that Basil Murphy could not have negotiated the stairs and nooks and crannies of even a well-monitored hotel was not as firm as it seemed?

Carrero looked up when Basil swung into the study on crutches but immediately subdued any surprise he felt. He said, "Don't you have your chair here?"

"You've seen me on crutches before."

Carrero did not answer, suggesting to Kim that he had not. She thought the lawyer incapable of admitting anything that might be construed as a deficiency on his part.

"What do you think of my hide-out?!"

"Not much. You would have been wiser to return to your apartment from the motel."

"I wanted to consult you first."

"I am in the book, Basil."

"And I don't want to be booked. The police want to talk to me about that despicable ass Conroy. I would rather speak to my lawyer on my own terms."

Carrero would not let it go. "We could have spoken in the motel. Or at my office. At your office." His eyes drifted to the wall behind Emtee Dempsey. "Alone."

Basil Murphy laughed. "Remy, did you watch the program Sister Mary Teresa appeared on?"

"Not yet."

"Then we must arrange a private showing. I have embargoed it for further broadcast. Sister was an extremely adroit participant. Until Conroy decided to launch a personal attack on me, she more than kept him on the defensive."

"I felt at a decided disadvantage," Emtee Dempsey said. "As I do now. I was wrong to bring you together here in my study. You have things to discuss and quite rightly do not want alien ears listening in."

Basil Murphy shook his head. "We have nothing to discuss. That is, if the advice is that I talk to the police. I would just as soon get that over with. Downstairs I watched a rerun of my show and I am anxious to get back to my office. Why should I be on the run?"

"Your life was threatened."

He looked at Emtee Dempsey. "Not for the first time."

"You're right, Basil," Carrero said. "We should speak to the police."

That, as it turned out, did not require leaving the house. The doorbell sounded and a minute later Richard Moriarity hurried down the hall to the study.

He paused in the doorway, taking in the scene: one handicapped celebrity and a lawyer he doubtless knew. And clearly he was anxious to speak with them both. And here they both were. The sight of Basil Murphy lolling in

Emtee Dempsey's study caused Richard's jaw to swell. It reminded him of other times when he had had the understandable feeling that Emtee Dempsey was interfering in his work. But he managed not to lose his temper.

"We are anxious to talk with you, Mr. Murphy."

Carrero spoke. "We were just about to contact you, Lieutenant." The lawyer advanced on Richard with extended hand. "This should save us all a lot of time. I'm sure there is somewhere in the house where we can speak confidentially."

"How long have you been here?" Richard asked Basil Murphy. He wanted to know if his quarry had been in the house while he had previously spoken with Emtee Dempsey. The answer soothed him until he began to wonder if he should believe it.

"I think we will all be much more comfortable in the living room," Emtee Dempsey said, pushing back from her desk. "Richard, give me your arm."

What a wheedler she was. Imagine, asking Richard for help in getting around in her own house. But he obeyed instinctively and, leaning on his arm, Emtee Dempsey led the parade into the living room. Carrero followed, trying to protest this arrangement without, however, sounding overly concerned. Murphy seemed more amused than anything by Carrero's discomfort. He accepted his crutches from Kim and followed the lawyer, his useless legs a mockery, but his upper body seeming more powerful than ever. The crutches emphasized the width of his shoulders as the wheelchair did not. Feeling superfluous, but curious, Kim went into the living room with the others.

Carrero made an effort to establish his authority once

everyone was seated, but Emtee Dempsey brushed aside the suggestion that they get right down to business. After all, this was her house and they were her guests. Was there anything in the way of refreshment that could be gotten for anyone? Richard's request for beer was followed by Basil Murphy's remark that he could use some solid food. Kim was sent to tell Joyce to make sandwiches and tea for three.

"Are we on a fast, or what?"

"For us too, of course. She's only counting guests. I'll make something for myself, Joyce."

"She'll want you in there, won't she? What's going on, anyway? I gather it's a little early for her to name Conroy's murderer."

"He may be in the living room," Kim said.

"Richard?"

Carrero was speaking when Kim returned to the living room. "Lieutenant, Mr. Murphy need not answer any questions unless you provide some valid reason for his doing so. My advice must be..."

Richard ignored him. "Mr. Murphy, have you ever been in Melvin Conroy's suite in the Claremont Hotel?"

"Certainly not."

"You have never been in the Claremont?"

"To visit Conroy? Never."

Carrero chose indignation as his weapon. "Basil, please do not answer any more questions. You have no obligation to and I strongly advise you to keep silent."

"What the hell for? The question was did I ever go visit Conroy in the Claremont Hotel and the answer is no."

Richard glanced at Emtee Dempsey, who watched Basil Murphy intently as he spoke.

"Basil," Carrero said, "he is setting a trap for you. They have evidence you were in Conroy's room when he was killed."

Basil Murphy uttered a word that might have been appropriate response to the suspicion but was not in the best taste with Sister Mary Teresa seated across from him in the full regalia of the Order of Martha and Mary. She ignored the expletive.

She said, "Mr. Murphy, you should tell Lieutenant Moriarity of the threat on your life."

"Threat?" Richard's incredulous tone was perhaps due to the fact that it was Emtee Dempsey who had mentioned the threat.

"It's why I have been hard to find, Lieutenant."

"On Mr. Carrero's advice, isn't that right?" Emtee Dempsey said.

"My advice seems more honored in the breach than otherwise," Carrero said resignedly.

"Who threatened you?" Richard asked.

Basil Murphy let out a sort of sigh. "It's a long story."

"For God's sake, don't say more than you have to, Basil."

"A short version wouldn't make sense. My life was threatened. What help is that unless I say who was behind it?"

"Melvin Conroy?" Richard asked.

Basil Murphy's laughter was a trilling tenor that startled Joyce as she came in from the kitchen with a tray. Kim got up to help. "I'm glad everyone is having fun," Joyce whispered through clenched teeth. "Where should I put this?"

"The coffee table, I think," Emtee Dempsey said, as if she had heard Joyce's whisper. There was a happy lilt in the old nun's voice, as if she found Basil Murphy's laughter contagious.

"I suppose Conroy was mad enough to want to kill me after I humiliated him in front of witnesses. But he let off steam by writing that ridiculous account in the *Tribune*." He looked at Emtee Dempsey. "Despite what I said earlier, Sister, I had no fear of Melvin Conroy."

"It was not he who threatened you?"

"It was not his threat that sent me to the Hi Hat."

Richard said, "Did Conroy have reason to fear you? You must have been mad enough to kill him after that newspaper article."

"Mad enough to kill? How mad is that?"

"A little madder than when you wrestled him to the floor on the set of your show."

"Ah. You've watched the film."

"Just the end of the program. You handled him remarkably well."

"Flattery? Handling a jerk like Conroy requires very little skill."

Richard let the remark linger, looking significantly at Basil Murphy. Carrero exposed his palms and sighed. Kim half expected him to ask Joyce to bring water and a towel so he could officially wash his hands of this.

"You don't seem interested in the threat on my life," Murphy said, taking a plate from Joyce.

"By an anonymous caller?" Richard had gone to the table to select a sandwich. He shook his head at the offer of coffee. "I would still like a beer."

"While you're working, Richard?"

He smiled sweetly at Kim. "Only when I'm working."

"Just my point," Basil Murphy said. "What possible significance can such a call, taken by itself, have? None. Like anybody else in television, I get weirdo calls and letters every day. If I reacted to those, I'd have been on the funny farm years ago. You have to know my marital troubles to understand."

"Basil, Basil," Carrero said, then sat back with closed eyes.

Murphy's account was basically what they had already learned from Katherine Senski and Lorrie Rione. He kept any suggestion of self-pity from his story, conveying the impression, if anything, that he regarded himself as a fool for expecting fidelity from a woman. Whether this was a universal skepticism or had special reference to his disability, it would have been difficult to say. Kim tended to think he meant it without reference to his handicap. It was not an attractive outlook, but Basil Murphy's experience was not calculated to make him philosophical. In any case, the story was interrupted when a call came through for Richard. The room fell silent while he listened. He put a hand over the receiver.

"A girl named Lorrie Rione work for you, Murphy?"

"She did."

"What does that mean?"

"I fired her yesterday."

"Why?"

"Why do you ask?"

"Your producer, Rick Kettler, just reported her missing."

"Probably a stunt. Is that Rick on the phone?"

Richard shook his head. "Are you suggesting this is a hoax?"

"No. Of course not. I don't know that. But Lorrie is a very imaginative girl."

"What exactly did Kettler report?" Emtee Dempsey asked when Richard put down the phone.

"He was supposed to meet her and she didn't show up and when he checked where she lives, the place was torn up and she was gone."

Basil Murphy looked bewildered. "I don't get it."

"Why did you fire her?"

"That's another long story, Lieutenant."

Richard nodded. "Okay. Let me make a suggestion, Mr. Murphy. Why don't you and I go downtown—you can bring your lawyer along, of course—and get these long stories down on the record?"

"That's fine with me."

"Well, it isn't with me," Carrero said, getting to his feet. He had been nibbling on a sandwich, eating just the crust, and he put it on his plate as he rose. "Basil, you are acting directly contrary to my advice. I cannot countenance your volunteering to divulge anything and everything to interviewers who are, whether you recognize it or not, hostile to your best interests."

"Then don't come."

"Are you dismissing me?"

Basil looked at him. How many friends and retainers had drifted away during his recent months of declining fortunes? "Okay, Remy. I'm no longer your client. That's what you want, isn't it?"

Five

The murder of the notorious novelist Geoffrey Chaser after his appearance on the Basil Murphy Show—the tape was shown three times in the days following the finding of Conroy's body, Murphy's embargo ignored—the newspaper attack on Murphy by Conroy, and the fact that Murphy had been questioned by the police, whatever the human tragedies involved, was a press agent's dream.

The film clip of Basil Murphy entering the detective division with a somewhat sheepish Richard Moriarity at his side was shown on all the local news programs.

Along with footage of Sister Mary Teresa, the other survivor of the physical contretemps with which the show ended.

"I gather that Mr. Conroy's reaction was quite characteristic of him," she said in answer to one of the inane questions put her. "Certainly Mr. Murphy was not surprised by the personal attack, by which I mean the verbal attack, on him by my fellow guest. When the attack became physical, Mr. Conroy more than met his match in Mr. Murphy."

"Did he actually clamber over you to get at Murphy?"

"I had a ringside seat certainly."

Sister Mary Teresa refused to watch herself on the set in the sun porch and brushed aside Kim's and Joyce's congratulations on how well she had handled herself.

"Avarice, not vanity, is supposedly the vice of age. Please do not flatter me. I was asked some silly questions and gave some silly answers. The fact that thousands of people heard and saw me give them is neither here nor there."

What undeniably pleased the old nun was the appearance of Lorrie Rione at their door. Her smile was radiant, eclipsing her gawky figure and wiglike hairdo. She saved the good news until they were all together, Emtee Dempsey, Kim and Joyce, having hot chocolate in the kitchen.

"I've been hired back."

"I should think so," Emtee Dempsey snorted. "Such nonsense."

"Now, if my boss can stay out of jail, my future looks bright."

"Where on earth have you been? You seem to have scared Rick Kettler half to death."

Lorrie's blush was a wonder to behold and she smiled the wider. "That was nuts of him, calling the police."

"He said your place was torn up."

"So I'm not much of a housekeeper. I was trying to find Mr. Murphy."

"Where did you look?" Emtee Dempsey wanted to know.

"The obvious place. His wife."

"Aha."

"Don't think she is happy with what has been happening to him. I know it bothers her. I think even Mr. Murphy realized it. I figured she was still someone he would turn to when the going got really rough."

"And what did Mrs. Murphy have to say?"

"Mrs. Murphy," Lorrie repeated with a smile. "Do you know, we never called her that. No one did. She remained Nancy Shale, as if it were a professional name. Maybe it was because we didn't want Mrs. Basil Murphy on the credits."

"What did she say when you told her you thought Mr. Murphy might be with her?"

"She wanted to talk about Pablo. I tell you, she is the most self-centered woman I have ever met. When she worked like a dog on the show, I thought, wow, what a wife. But she considered the show her own. It was when it finally dawned on her that it remained Basil Murphy's Show no matter what she did that school was out. And Pablo was in. So when I go to her, worried sick about her husband, she starts to tell me her troubles with Pablo."

"What did you do?"

"Listen. Believe me, I had no choice. You have to know Nancy Shale."

In the shadow of the immense Water Tower stand a number of smaller buildings, one of which was the residential hotel where Melvin Conroy had lived. In another of these, a block away, the Estrella del Norte, Nancy Shale had taken an apartment when she moved out of Basil Murphy's. Kim had the impression that the rooms were not of appropriate dimensions for the woman who descended into the sunken living room, her light green dress flowing behind her, one hand just touching her necklace, a receptive expression on the tanned face framed by the famous silver hair. She wore glasses with massive lenses, and when she stopped she seemed to lean forward as if to see Kim better.

"I thought you said you were a nun."

"I am."

Nancy Shale looked Kim over. "Well, of course I know things have changed, but I am nonetheless surprised. I watched Basil's show with Sister Mary Teresa and what's-his-name. Oh, I know his name, but if I call him Conroy that seems silly, and the name he wrote under is sillier still."

"Sister Mary Teresa prefers to wear the traditional habit of our order. At her age it makes more sense."

Black eyebrows appeared above the glasses. "Meaning you're too young and pretty to conceal the fact?"

The blush that suffused Kim's face made her feel like Lorrie Rione at the mention of Rick Kettler.

"That isn't what I meant."

"Not what you meant to say, anyway." But the smile was gentle and Kim did not take further offense at being teased. In self-defense, a question had already formed on her lips. "How is Pablo?" Fortunately, she did not ask it. That would have been the end of the visit and Emtee Dempsey would have been unforgiving.

"It's because of Sister Mary Teresa that I'm here."

Nancy Shale Murphy seemed to float into a chair, a weightless object borne on gusts of wind. Except that Mrs. Murphy, unlike a falling leaf, seemed very much in control of her fate. "She is also the reason I agreed to see you."

Sister Mary Teresa would have preferred Nancy Shale to come to the house on Walton Street, but she pleaded a debilitating cold, no sign of which had put in an appearance. Was her nose red, perhaps? The tan made the question hard to answer. How did she keep such a tan in the middle of the Chicago winter? Kim suspected that Nancy Shale was privy to cosmetological secrets that would be forever unknown to her.

"She wants me to ask you some questions about Basil Murphy."

"Yes?"

"You know the police think your husband murdered Geoffrey Chaser?"

"Nonsense."

"Exactly Sister Mary Teresa's reaction. She feels a certain obligation to your husband..."

"Please don't call him that."

Kim inhaled and went on. "To Basil Murphy, then. Because she was there when the fight broke out."

"That's a pretty weak reason."

"Not to Sister Mary Teresa."

"She's just curious, isn't she?"

A conspiratorial smile. Just between us girls.

"I suppose everyone is curious to know who killed Geoffrey Chaser. Aren't you?"

"Not particularly. What I've heard of him makes it difficult to mourn him."

"Yes. But Sister Mary Teresa sat in the chair next to his. She talked with him. It is that that makes the difference."

Nancy Shale thought a minute, then conceded the point. "Perhaps. But if she doesn't think Basil did it, what help could I be?"

"He may not have done it, but obviously someone went to quite a bit of trouble to make it look as if he had."

"How so?"

"The police say they have evidence Basil Murphy was in Geoffrey Chaser's suite."

"Really? I don't remember seeing that in the paper."

"It wasn't in the paper."

"What kind of evidence do they have?"

"The imprint of the tire of his wheelchair."

"Is that all?"

"It proves he was there."

"At most it proves his wheelchair was there, if it proves that."

Kim could not keep from smiling.

"What's funny?"

"Sister Mary Teresa is going to be sorry she didn't get a chance to talk with you personally."

"I wouldn't want to give her this cold." A demonstrative snuffle that seemed genuine enough. "You're here at your own risk."

"I don't catch colds."

"I might have said the same thing a few days ago." She rubbed the bridge of her nose. "I'm not always a mouth breather. What did I say that would have won me the convent prize?"

"The fact that doubt can be cast on the police evidence only underscores the point. Who would want to point the finger of accusation at Basil Murphy?"

A little gasp. "How stupid of me."

Kim said nothing.

"She thinks I had something to do with it, doesn't she?"

"Did you?"

Emtee Dempsey insisted on direct questions when she had to rely on Kim as intermediary. And Kim was to be alert to every aspect of reaction to such questions. A series of expressions flickered across Nancy Shale's face and Kim was suddenly struck by the almost leathery texture of the older woman's skin. Was that the price she paid for her tan? Surprise and anger, finally amusement, showed on her tanned face.

"Will she accept my denial?"

"Are you denying it?"

A half smile took possession of the right side of her mouth. "Tell her I said No Comment."

"You're making it impossible for her not to speak with you personally."

"You should have brought her along."

"Would you go back with me?"

"Not today, my dear."

Behind her, on the level of the dining room, which from the living room took on the aspect of a stage, a young man appeared. His great mane of hair was worn long in a style Kim thought had passed; his striped shirt, sleeves rolled to the elbow, unbuttoned to the navel, was pushed loosely into washed-out jeans. His feet were bare. At the sight of Kim, he paused and seemed to assume a pose, like that of a male model. Kim's expression caused Nancy Shale to turn.

"Ta tum," she intoned. "And here, direct from Las Vegas, is the incredible, the sensational..." She turned to Kim. "But maybe you don't know Pablo."

If Nancy Shale had glided into the room, Pablo came bounding down to their level, his bare feet losing themselves in the deep pile of the rug. "Sorry to break in." But there was no sorrow in his voice or on his face. His mouth seemed excessively full of very large teeth when he smiled at Kim. "Who's got a cigarette?"

Nancy pushed a porcelain box toward him. "Pablo, this is Sister Kimberly. Sister, Pablo Quince, the entertainer."

"En-ter-tain-er?" He looked at Nancy while he lit a cigarette and then turned to Kim. "Sister."

"As in convent," Nancy Shale explained.

Pablo Quince bowed and made a parody of the sign of the cross over his thin chest.

It was one of those moments Kim had to face from time to time, and it brought home to her how protected her life was, by and large. She might not wear the habit, but she could still count on the traditional respect shown to nuns in the situations in which she usually found herself. Wearing ordinary clothes was meant to break down barriers, but it also removed protections, primarily the unconscious assumption that her vocation and status would be shown deference. With Pablo Quince, this was far from predictable, and Kim had an intimation that Nancy Shale would not come to her aid if Pablo decided to be embarrassing.

"Sister Kimberly seems unimpressed by the apple of so many teen-agers' eyes."

Pablo took this for an invitation. He held his cigarette affectedly in one hand, put the other on his hip, and began to gyrate slowly as a sort of groaning began to issue from his lips. It turned into something like singing, but the better part of his effort was put into bodily movements, a male ecdysiast. In embarrassment, more for Quince than for herself, Kim turned her eyes to Nancy Shale. The older woman's face glowed as she followed the movements of the young man's body. Mouth-breather, indeed. Abruptly, Pablo stopped, took a drag on his cigarette, and looked expectantly at his audience. Nancy Shale's eyes met Kim's and the sudden leap of shame did something to redeem her in Kim's eyes.

Bursting once more into song, Pablo slunk from the room. The young man's music was little more than erotic excitation and Kim was suddenly aware how sympathetic she was with Emtee Dempsey's condemnation of contemporary popular music, citing Plato, Aristotle, and the *Motu Proprio* of Pius XI on liturgical music. Sometimes there were references to Kierkegaard as well. The musical erotic. Kim had told herself she would check out these allusions. Maybe this brief exposure—somehow that seemed the appropriate word—to Pablo Quince would provide the decisive motive. Not only the beat of such music, but also the lyrics, were said to be the most overt appeal to the basest instincts. Worse, it was aimed at subteen-agers and thus represented a deliberate corrupting of youth. That such animal rhythms should also affect a woman of Nancy Shale's age and intelligence was a genuine surprise. What little of such music Kim heard, before she or Joyce could lunge at the radio and turn the dial, seemed a penance to the ear.

No melody, no lifting of the soul, just a sonic thumping that was like a physical assault.

"You don't like him," Nancy Shale said.

"But you do."

Nancy Shale flipped open the cigarette box and took one. She looked at it a moment before putting it into her mouth. "I've taken up smoking again. Why not make a complete fool of myself?"

Kim did not comment.

"I left Basil Murphy for that boy. Boy. How old would you say he is?"

"I've no idea."

"But you know he's younger than I am."

"He is younger than I am too."

That seemed to surprise Nancy Shale. "I suppose he could be. How old are you?"

"Would you answer that question?"

"Not in the circumstances, no." She crushed out her cigarette as if wanting to end the discussion. But then she looked up and said, "So you've been sent to find out who I think might want to do Basil in? One answer would be, thousands of people. Success attracts hatred. Did you know that? People profoundly resent it when someone does well by doing something well. I used to think it had something to do with democracy gone mad—equality before and after the race is won—but I think it is more universal than that, certainly not just American. Americans hate success. Or rather, they hate the successful. We're all meant to be successful, aren't we? But only some make it. No wonder we hate them." A smile. "End of lecture. Basil is very good at what he does and deservedly successful. Yet his mail contains truly venomous letters." She began to shake her head. "But Sister Mary Teresa won't be satisfied with that, will she? Okay. Suspect number one." Again the little smile. "A lawyer named Remy Carrero."

"We've met him."

"Where?"

"He came to the house. I didn't like him."

"He is a viper. He led Basil and me and a few others into some extremely bad investments. It's no fun to lose money, but to be treated like a crook as well is too much. I doubt that Remy lost any of his money."

"How long has he been Basil Murphy's lawyer?"

"Since before we met. I say that with some measure of pride. He is not my doing. I distrusted him from the start, and vice versa. But I thought it would look bitchy if I tried to dislodge all Basil's friends. Acquaintances. Basil doesn't have friends."

Kim looked surprised.

"Think of it, Sister. Handicapped like that. Living at a perpetual disadvantage. For the most part, people patronized or ignored him. Why shouldn't he distrust motivation when deference is shown him—after he is successful? I had a helluva time overcoming that myself. He was sure it was pity or some effort to get my hands on his money. Anything but the simple fact that I liked and admired him. I did and I do." She lit another cigarette. "So why do I give him the shaft when he's down on his luck? Well, if it made sense, I might have a reason. But it doesn't. I'm being a damned fool. It won't last with Pablo. I know it and I love it." She shrugged. "Maybe you're still woman enough to understand."

It was one of Emtee Dempsey's observations that most of what is good but, more important, most of what is bad in human life can be traced to sex. She said this as a mere matter of fact, without condescension or condemnation. "I thank God for my vocation, Sisters. Much that is good is put behind us forever when we enter religion. Not that we are free from temptation, but by and large the thing that plagues most human lives is not a factor in ours. This is a great blessing. There is no surer proof of Original Sin than the fact that human beings have made such a mess of the means of procreation and loving intimacy. We live in an age that dreads sex and holds it in contempt. Pornography is a diabolical rejection of the importance of sex. It seeks to demean and dishonor it. To mock it. I say this because our life is sometimes regarded as a retreat from reality. But it is the worldly who are blind to reality."

Such a homily could be prompted by many things, a blur of magazine covers on their morning walk to and from the cathedral, a minute or two spent watching comedians, male and female, on late-night talk shows. The continuous background snickering about sex suggested an unhealthy obsession.

But where did that put Nancy Shale? Kim felt sorry for the woman, acting like a fool and knowing it, unable to be guided by her own best judgment. Her frankness seemed to separate her from the type Emtee Dempsey found almost beyond hope.

"Okay," Nancy said, flicking ash from her cigarette. "There's Remy. Sister Mary Teresa has met him so she can figure him out for herself. Me? Well, why would I do such a thing to Basil? You will be told that my sister Sheilah

~ 99 ~

might. She and Greg—Gregorovius, her husband—tended to blame Basil rather than Carrero for getting them into the tax shelter that wasn't.The people who work for Basil? They worship him. Probably more so now than when I ran things." She blew smoke contemplatively at the ceiling. "I wonder if Basil will take me back when Pablo tires of me?"

From another room the sound of the putative singing of the rock star became audible. It seemed a note on which to go. Kim felt she had the main thing she had come for, the unlikelihood that Basil Murphy's wife was at the bottom of his troubles. Nancy Shale tried to conceal how happy she was that Kim was going. Descending in the elevator, Kim thought that, all other considerations aside, she would not have been attracted to Pablo Quince if he were the last man—or boy—on earth. Poor Nancy Shale Murphy.

Katherine Senski and Emtee Dempsey were huddled in the study when Kim returned, and she was asked to join them. Neither of the older women brought her up to date, just went on with their conversation, but eventually Kim was able to put things together.

While she had been looking into the possibility that Nancy Shale was worth pursuing as the one causing Basil Murphy trouble, Emtee Dempsey had enlisted Katherine to pursue another spoor: Geoffrey Chaser's literary connections.

"In a manner of speaking," Emtee Dempsey said, rolling her eyes.

Katherine had produced a written document, and the list of names was a trifle daunting.

In first place was Abner Singleton, the literary agent whose idea it had been to take the paperback novel Geoffrey Chaser had sold for two thousànd dollars but that refused to go out of print, and interest a hardback publisher in it and future Geoffrey Chaser products. He had, in a word, turned Conroy into a millionaire. With the customary caution of the literary agent, he had written himself into the contracts he negotiated for Conroy/Chaser. All royalties were paid to Singleton and he in turn, having taken his ten per cent, paid the rest to Conroy. Standard practice, which provides the author with bookkeeping services and an accurate account of his earnings. Like most authors, Conroy had come to resent the role his agent played. After all, he wrote the books and what could Abner Singleton do without those? The agent took on the aspect of a parasite, feeding undeservedly off the sweat of Melvin Conroy's brow. He began a long and unsuccessful campaign to get Singleton to reduce his commission from ten to five per cent. There was no general agreement between author and agent, of course, and Conroy was thus able to act as his own agent in the sale of his last two books. He was still bound to Singleton by the contracts for previous books, but now he was on his own. And, as dumb luck would have it, the movie sales, which had always eluded Abner Singleton's considerable skill, now materialized. Conroy, on his own, negotiated a remarkable film contract that included rights to his total previous production. Which, of course, meant that, willy-nilly, Conroy was going to have to pay ten per cent of the movie profits from the books the contracts of which Singleton had negotiated. Equally, of course, he did not want to do this. He refused.

Singleton took him to court. The case was pending. Abner Singleton had little doubt that his claim would be upheld, but the fact that he had to make it, that it would cost him money to get money that was already rightly his, led the normally laconic agent to speak of Conroy in terms Nero had reserved for Christians.

"So, Sisters, Abner Singleton could conceivably have eased Melvin Conroy from this vale of tears."

"And attempted to divert attention to Basil Murphy?"

Katherine could not say. "Let us leave that as a separate question."

"Ah," said Emtee Dempsey. "Good girl."

Before turning to those who had unwillingly provided a basis for one of Geoffrey Chaser's novels, Katherine drew attention to Conroy's publishers, both hardback and paperback. The former meant his editor, Glen Regensburg, whose connection with the quasi-pornography of Melvin Conroy had mystified the book world. Every other author with whom Regensburg worked had a genuine claim to literary accomplishment. Why should he sully himself with the likes of Geoffrey Chaser? The best available answer was that there lurks in the breast of even the most honorable of men a secret desire to act like a rogue. Melvin Conroy, as Geoffrey Chaser, had provided Regensburg that chance, he had taken it, and he dismissed all criticism with a smile and a twinkle in his eye doubtless meant to be roguish. And then Conroy had turned on him. Not quite saying Regensburg had urged him to turn his novels into the sort of sleaze they were, but implying it, Conroy had managed to convey the charge in such a way that it was all but impossible for Regensburg to answer it. Except to resign as Conroy's editor. But Conroy would not permit this. He threatened the publisher to take his books elsewhere if anyone other than Regensburg were assigned as his editor. Pressure was exerted from above and, in a way not unlike those between author and agent, relations between Conroy and his editor were strained.

"Is he here in Chicago?"

"Not normally, no. But when an author makes as much money for a house as Conroy does, the mountain comes to Mohammed. Conroy has been summoning poor Regensburg from New York regularly, out of spite. For that matter, Abner Singleton's office is in New York. But both men were caught in Chicago by the snow, here to talk with Conroy, Regensburg directly, Singleton via the editor."

"Well, well."

But if the editor and agent were thus not without motives for wishing to see the last of Melvin Conroy, the victims of his pen had stronger motives still. There were, as Conroy liked to boast, nine of them in all. It helped that only four had been in Chicago at the time of Conroy's murder.

One of the four was Madelaine Marr, the saintly lady who for years had lived on State Street, ministering to the desperate and degenerate. In her early years she had been given to making remarks about the objects of her concern that suggested they were victims, but her conversion to Catholicism had rid her work of political and social overtones. That people are sometimes victims, she did not of course deny, but those she met daily had no one to blame but themselves for their present plight. "If alcoholism is a disease," she had said, in a remark that raised an eyebrow or two, "it is responsibly contracted." Was this new approach taken with an eye to more frequent changes in the woebegone types who showed up at the door of what was called simply The House? Madelaine Marr had been engaged in her work long enough to know that it is very rare for human beings to make fundamental changes in their lives, especially changes for the better. It was the chance of mercy and forgiveness, of a life beyond the present, that had become for her the only intelligible reason for doing what she was doing. And of course making the present less awful by providing food and shelter to the endless army of men at the end of their ropes.

Her longtime companion in her work was the editor of the mimeographed newsletter who, now that political and sociological explanations had been abandoned, concentrated on prodding comfortable Christians to see that their lives were in some ways as desperate as those of the denizens of The House. Jorge Higgins, a transplanted Argentine, once a wino, was now a teetotaler who explained the dramatic change in his life by pointing upward as he grinned at the inquirer. To say that Jorge felt loyalty to Madelaine Marr would be on the level of saying that Charles Lindbergh had possessed daring. Toward all else in this world he had adopted a mildly amused attitude, but he could countenance no criticism of Madelaine. Since there was no criticism of her, this truth had been hidden until the publication of *Gruel Treatment*. The pages of the newsletter became eloquent with a call for a champion with money who could sue the author and remove all doubt about the good name of Madelaine Marr. What particularly hurt Jorge was the fact that when Geoffrey

Chaser, identifying himself simply as Mel Conroy, journalist—as if anyone at The House would have recognized the pen name—came asking about The House and its foundress, Jorge had willingly spent hours telling anecdotes of their work. Some of these, given an utterly gratuitous twist, made their way into the book that Jorge read as if it were a Lenten penance.

Madelaine had not read the book. She was totally indifferent to its existence or to any effect it might have. None of the derelicts she helped was likely to read a book, and they were the central concern of her life. She had smiled away Conroy's questions. Perhaps, after years of prayer and good works, she had her Master's intuition where Judas was concerned. Quite apart from that possibility, she refused as a matter of policy to talk about herself, though to call it a policy made it sound calculated. She put Conroy to work preparing vegetables for the daily stew and that had taken care of that.

When the book appeared, sympathetic reporters came to elicit condemnations from her, but without success. Someone had portrayed her as a sinner? She could hardly take exception to that. She was a sinner. "As are we all." No unction, no pious dropping of the eyes, no saccharine smile. She was simply stating the truth.

She was a thin, rawboned woman whose gray hair was braided and worn wrapped round her head. Her eyes were sunken and seemed in possession of some truth the rest of us seek in vain. Her hands were large and red, the hands of a washerwoman. She looked like a photograph of a woman in the dustbowl during the Depression. She had been born to money, she had been educated at Radcliffe, she had lived a radical youth and written poetry of a defiant Edna St. Vincent Millay sort. It had been at three o'clock one morning when, returning through deserted streets from a party, she had come upon a man quite literally lying in the gutter. "Jesus," her companion had said in disgust. To help the derelict assumed the nature of an imperative she could not resist, and from that day to the present she had been doing the same.

Not a very likely murderer of Melvin Conroy.

The three others were more quickly described by Katherine in her written report, and each seemed a plausible murderer.

1. James Oliver Hawk, restaurateur, whose El Comedor catered to affluent Chicagoans in a north-shore location that defied the zoning laws. Short, portly, punctilious, and very much on his dignity, Hawk was an obsequious host who provided an undeniably peerless cuisine and whose establishment had for years been the unquestioned ultimate stop of a night on the town for the beautiful and wealthy. Who knows the magic of such reputations? Katherine Senski did not. True, Hawk personally invited celebrities and notables visiting Chicago to dine at El Comedor, compliments of its admiring owner. The certainty that Someone would be at El Comedor was part of the explanation of its popularity. Perhaps everyone was there to see everyone else. And then *The Bitten Hand* appeared. James Oliver Hawk, as Osvaldo Bussard, stripped of his charm and elegance and genuine gift for creating an atmosphere of excitement, came through as a craven bootlick whose adulation for the elite was a mask behind which he avenged himself on them in various ways. A recent un-

solved string of burglaries on the Gold Coast was traced, in Geoffrey Chaser's imagination, to Hawk—or Bussard—as Fagan. And who was the source of hostile comments in the gossip columns of the Chicago papers? None other than Bussard. Who else could possibly know as much?

When the book appeared, the identification with Hawk was made not only in the book reviews but also in the gossip columns—with denials. Hawk made the mistake of turning it into a cause célèbre, and journalists, wittingly or not, cooperated in his folly. Within six months El Comedor was just another club restaurant, barely breaking even. Hawk had lost weight, he brooded, drank too much, and took on the look of a man desperate for revenge.

2. Philip Canaris, the Chicago novelist whose national, even international, reputation was firmly founded on genius and genuine literary accomplishment, was unlikely to be linked in anyone's mind with Geoffrey Chaser. Canaris was a novelist; Chaser was a bad joke on the book world. But Melvin Conroy could not abide the prominence accorded Canaris and the fact that it was Canaris, not he, who was *the* Chicago novelist. Did Conroy think the trash he wrote was on the same level as Canaris's? Perhaps he felt, and who can say without reason, that he might have used his own talents honestly and produced work deserving of comparison with that of Canaris. But it was Canaris who had reputation and honor, while Conroy, under a pen name, had only notoriety—and wealth—as a result of his writing. Conroy did, at least fitfully, try to see himself as the legitimate heir of the great popular and prolific novelists of the nineteenth century. In this mood, the writing of Canaris could seem to him effete and mannered, written

for a clique of critics, not for flesh-and-blood readers.

In *The Importance of Being Ernest,* he contrasted the kind of writer he took Canaris to be with a Hemingway redivivus, obviously meant to be himself. The manhood of the novelist he named Birdsong was called into question, but the claim that his best work was imitation bordering on plagiarism constituted the nub of the attack. What made it devastating was the fact that Conroy, under his own name, wrote a piece for a Chicago newspaper's Sunday magazine in which he drew attention to the amazing similarity between passages in Canaris's second novel and the third chapter of *The Great Gatsby.* The passages in Canaris's *Easeful Death* reproduced the rhythms of the juxtaposed passages from Fitzgerald, the syntactical and rhetorical similarities were, to say the least, amazing, and the occurrence of three unusual words—cadenza, recusant, and verdant—in both passages made the article impossible for Canaris to ignore.

To say that his reply was weak would be kind. He congratulated Conroy for seeing what other critics had missed. The passage in question was a deliberate imitation, not to say parody. He had been mindful of Joyce's *Ulysses* when he wrote *Easeful Death.* There were other such parodies of other authors in the book and Canaris invited the interested to find them. But what was discovered were dozens of instances of dependencies on Fitzgerald's *The Great Gatsby.* No other parodies were found and Canaris himself was unable to point them out. Conroy's parting shot was the challenge that others find the books from which Canaris had borrowed his other successes. Nothing had appeared from the pen of Phillip Canaris since this episode.

3. Phonsie Quilmes, née Alphonsine Brady, Chicago athlete, Silver Medalist in the Pan-American games, Bronze Medalist in the Olympics, who had switched from swimming to golf, played in the LPGA for four years, and then settled down as teaching professional at the Calumet Club overlooking the lake, was another victim. She was a successful woman, seemingly invulnerable to the sort of sleazy attack a Geoffrey Chaser might mount, but the novelist had an uncanny sense of the weakness concealed beneath strength. He knew too that the objective importance of a person's Achilles' heel is of little or no importance. It is rather the significance attached to it by the person involved. He discovered Phonsie's weakness in an old episode, antedating her appearance in the Olympics, the final match in which she had won the women's state amateur title in golf. At this time, golf was little more than an avocation, relief from swimming, but her natural grace and ability put her at the top of any field she chose to enter. And there she was, freckle-faced and blue-eyed, squinting against a long-ago sun as she was captured by the camera. Thus she squinted out at Conroy when he read the old accounts. Her opponent had accused Phonsie of cheating by improving her lie in a fairway bunker. There had been a twenty-four-hour flap, the accuser said she had been mistaken, and the single cloud on the otherwise sunny landscape of Phonsie's athletic career drifted away. Until Geoffrey Chaser, in *What Do You Lie?*, resurrected the thing. His character Flossie Wilmette is accused of a similar misdemeanor and buys off her accuser.

The number of people likely to link that fictional account with the actual history of Phonsie Quilmes was, by any objective estimate, small. Minuscule. But those few were precisely the people whose good opinion was essential to Phonsie's self-esteem, peace of mind, and generally exuberant outlook. Who brought the novel to her attention? Why, the author, of course. A gift copy, complete with an equivocal dedication. "For Phonsie Quilmes, may none of your strokes be cardiac and all your lies be favorable." The scrawled signature was that of Melvin Conroy, in case she did not know. Her reaction was completely out of proportion to the importance of the event, objectively speaking. But an athlete's reputation is part of her sinew, bone, marrow, psyche. Phonsie had been attacked in the single way that could hurt her.

Nothing if not direct, she went to confront the author. She found him in a downtown grill having lunch. It was a place frequented by media people. Phonsie gripped Conroy's shirtfront and lifted him out of his chair. It was completely physical and completely silent. She looked him in the eye with contempt and then shoved him forward into his lunch.

The event was as much reported as any of her athletic triumphs had been, but it did not work in her favor. Vague thoughts about freedom of the press clouded the minds of witnesses and they, however reluctantly, rose to Conroy's defense. And the seed of doubt was planted about Phonsie's athletic ability. It did not matter that three weeks before, crowding forty, she had effortlessly won the city title for the seventh time. The subsequent effect on her was horrendous. She was heard to say she should have maimed the bastard when she had her hands on him. She was heard to say that she did not understand why Conroy had not been snuffed years ago. It was true that she said this after several whiskey sours, but the whiskey sours were new and seemed a further sign of her fall from grace.

Emtee Dempsey liked things neat. She liked lists. She liked summaries, particularly her own. She liked problems defined, analyzed, broken into their parts, and handled in logical order. She was manifestly pleased with the portraits that had been put before her. She congratulated Katherine Senski. She smiled at Kim. She looked at the ceiling with a thoughtful expression.

"I suppose the police will already have spoken with these people." She shook her headdress impatiently. "Of course they have. No reason for us to duplicate their efforts. What we must first do is find out from Richard what they have learned."

Kim said, keeping her face expressionless, "He may not be eager to confide in you, Sister."

"I should think not. But his sister, Sister?"

"Even less. What possible reason could I give?"

A beatific smile came and went on Emtee Dempsey's face, the kind of smile Fra Angelico caught for his cherubim. She brought her pudgy hands together in an attitude of prayer.

"You can wonder aloud if what he has found matches what I have learned."

Six

A puzzle dear to logicians concerns a shipwrecked man who stumbles ashore on a strange island where he encounters a native who tells him, "On this island we always lie." The beached logician forgets his hunger and thirst as he considers that, if the man is telling the truth, not everyone on the island always lies and thus what he says must be a lie. On the other hand...

Katherine held up her hand. "Sister Mary Teresa, if you please. This is not a classroom and I am not an undergraduate. What has this to do with your suggestion to Sister Kimberly?"

Emtee Dempsey looked hurt. "I am addressing myself to the startling remark that I asked her to lie. The telling of lies is abhorrent to me. It is never morally permissible to lie. If there is any ethical absolute I embrace with fervor it is that one. I would never counsel another to tell a lie."

"Just to mislead others?"

"My dear Sister Kimberly, if we are to be held account-able for every interpretation and misinterpretation others put on our words and actions, then may God indeed have mercy on our souls. We are all doomed."

On occasions like this it was essential, Kim knew, to stick to the point at issue. If allowed to manage the field, Emtee Dempsey would soon have them agreeing that Up is Down.

"You want me to suggest to Richard that you have found out something relevant to the murder of Melvin Conroy?"

"Exactly!"

Kim expected to be told to go to the head of the class. "Have you?"

"Indeed I have."

"What?" The interrogative popped from Kim's mouth in exasperation.

"But, Sister, you know everything I know. And surely you will agree that we know a good deal more now than we did a day or two ago."

"But if I tell Richard what you want, he will think you know who killed Melvin Conroy."

"Yes."

"But you can't let him think that. You can't deceive him like that."

"Sister Kimberly, I would be a very stupid person in-deed if I had no idea who the murderer is."

"Who?"

"To name a person now would seem slanderous. I need to know a bit more before I name names."

"Who is it?" Katherine said, sitting forward.

It was a measure of Emtee Dempsey's power that both Kim and Katherine half thought the old nun did know who killed Melvin Conroy. But there was no way she could know, Kim assured herself. She couldn't if she knew only what Kim knew. Could she? Kim found it difficult to discard the possibility completely. That, of course, was what the old nun was counting on with Richard. How could he be sure, after past performances, that Emtee Dempsey could not blithely say, "But obviously X did it, Richard?"

Emtee Dempsey waved away the argument that it could scarcely be slander to name someone here in the privacy of her study on Walton Street. Katherine Senski narrowly escaped a little homily on the nature of slander, but she was saved by her inspired suggestion.

"Very well, write down the name of the murderer and later, when everything is clear, show me what you wrote."

Without hesitation, Emtee Dempsey put a clean piece of paper before her, uncapped her large fountain pen, and wrote in her firm hand. She folded the paper twice, put it into an envelope and sealed it. "Where would you like me to keep this, Katherine?"

Kim had to admire the old nun's sense of drama. She herself was dying to know what name had been written on the sheet of paper, if Emtee Dempsey had indeed written a name. She was equally certain that when the time came Emtee Dempsey would produce the envelope. With this dramatic gesture she had put her reputation on the line, perhaps not as publicly as in the past, but decisively, nonetheless. She would never attempt to deceive Katherine Senski.

"Now, Sister Kimberly, will you contact your brother? No, that is not the way to put it. I do not mean to suggest that you, like Katherine, wished to put me to the test. But I have been put to the test, so you can dismiss your groundless reluctance to speak to Richard. You can tell him what I have done. If only for that reason, I welcomed Katherine's dare."

"Where did she put the envelope?" Joyce asked when Kim told her what had happened. Kim had taken her coat into the kitchen in preparation for going out.

"Surely you don't think she would lie."

"No. But I'd like to see what she wrote."

"The envelope is in her desk drawer."

Of course neither of them would look. Sister Mary Teresa knew that. It was this kind of simple trust that made her so hard to understand. Hers was a very complex simplicity, but finally it had to be granted that she hadn't a bad bone in her body.

"I don't believe it," Richard said.

"I don't know who she thinks did it, she wouldn't tell me, but she assured both Katherine Senski and me that she knows the name of the murderer."

"And you believed her?"

"Do the police know who did it?"

The question chased the mocking smile from his face, a face that was the masculine version of Kim's own, lean, a little too pale with the red hair, very blue eyes. Angry eyes, at the moment.

"Kim, there are procedures we ordinary mortals go through when faced with a murder. We don't sit around in convent parlors playing guessing games. We gather evidence, we interview people, we move only as fast as a responsible investigation permits..."

"No leads at all?"

"Leads! My God, there are lots of leads. You met the guy. Conroy. Half of Chicago would have liked to throw him in the lake wearing a concrete overcoat. We are engaged in an enormous task of elimination."

"I think that was Emtee Dempsey's method too."

Richard would never strike a woman, but Kim was his sister and it looked for a moment as if he were going to make a sibling exception to the rule.

"Okay, who's her suspect?"

"I don't know."

"Come on, Kim."

"I mean it. She wouldn't say who it was, but she did write down the name."

"Wrote it down? What kind of game were you playing?"

"Then she put the paper in an envelope and sealed it. She put it in her desk."

Richard was hooked now. She felt as she had when they were kids fishing at Wolf Lake and there was the tug at the line that meant she had a catch. She reeled Richard in with merciful quickness, once she had him. But she saw in his eyes a dozen schemes forming to get that piece of paper and see what the impossible old woman had written down.

"I don't have time for this," he said as they went out to the Volkswagen.

"Richard, you don't have to come if you don't want to."
"I should drive myself."

He said this as he pulled open the passenger door of the VW and eased himself into the cramped space. "These things were made for midgets."

"No, by midgets. In the Black Forest. Or was it elves?"

The motor, unoffended by this banter, started on the first twist of the key. How could you malign a car that started so faithfully in the midst of a Chicago winter?

What Richard found out at Walton Street was not the name Emtee Dempsey had written down and put away in her desk. He found out there had been another murder.

Kim slid into a parking place beside a snowdrift half again as high as the Volkswagen, but before they got out Joyce appeared beside the car, tapping on the window with a bare hand. She was not wearing a coat. Kim rolled down the frosted window and looked out at Joyce shivering in the street, hugging herself.

"What in heaven's name are you doing?"

"Kim, something awful has happened. Headquarters wants Richard right away."

Richard leaned across. "What happened?"

But Joyce looked at Kim. "He's dead, Kim. Basil Murphy is dead."

"Good Lord."

Richard barked, "Where the hell do they want me to go?"

"WRZR."

"Let's go, let's go," Richard urged, and without hesitating, Kim put the car in gear and headed off into the twilight, bound once again for the station.

In some ways the trip was easier this time, in some

ways it was worse. The weather was not what it had been, the streets were cleared and salted, the traffic was not too heavy. But now she had Richard beside her instead of Emtee Dempsey, Richard angry that she did not go faster, Richard angry that he had not taken his own car when they left his office, Richard wondering if he shouldn't flag down a patrol car and continue that way.

"It's perfectly all right with me. Where's a patrol car?"

"I'll keep an eye out."

Where is a patrol car when you need one? After they had gone two thirds of the distance to the station Richard forgot about looking for patrol cars and slumped, to the degree that he could, in his seat and glowered at the road ahead. Kim preferred him grumbling. It kept her mind off the reason for this long drive.

Basil Murphy dead. It was difficult to believe.

"Who do you suppose..."

"Let's wait till we get there."

Rebuffed, Kim spoke in order to wound him in turn. "There goes your number one suspect."

"I never really thought he did it. But we had to check him out because of..." He stopped. Why should he explain anything to her, a mere woman and his sister besides? Two strikes right there against her.

"Maybe Conroy killed Murphy," Kim suggested.

"Funny."

"That would be neat, wouldn't it? Conroy slips Murphy a slow-acting poison, Murphy strangles Conroy..."

"Shut up. Please."

"We cab drivers like to talk to our clients."

"A cab would have been quicker."

"It's not too late."

He shut up and so did she. She had arrived at WRZR. She did not deposit him at the front door as she had Emtee Dempsey. Having come this far, she intended to stick with him. Emtee Dempsey would have to wait for her report on Richard's reaction to her gambit. All that seemed somehow silly now, anyway, with Basil Murphy dead.

Richard was out of the car and sprinting across the parking lot to the entrance of WRZR before Kim could get out of the car. When she herself reached the entrance she found that all but one door to the right of the revolving doors were locked and it was by no means certain she would be allowed to enter.

"I'm with Lieutenant Moriarity."

The uniformed cop looked skeptical.

"Sorry, Miss. No unauthorized personnel."

"You mean I can go?" Kim smiled brightly. "Oh, good. Tell Lieutenant Moriarity you told me to go, okay?"

"Wait a minute..."

But Kim turned and skipped down the steps and started back to her car with the sound of the cop's shouting following her. He caught up to her as she pretended to have trouble with the door.

"I thought you were guarding the entrance," she said accusingly.

He looked back at the untended door. "Don't worry about that," he said worriedly. "I can keep an eye on it from here. Now, just who are you?"

"I don't see what business that is of yours."

"You mentioned Lieutenant Moriarity."

"Yes, we came here together."

"Come back with me, then, and we'll find the lieutenant."

It was ruses like this that provided Emtee Dempsey with some of the keenest enjoyment in her life, but Kim did not have the dramatic flair to want to carry the act beyond the purpose she had had for beginning it. Not that it would not have been fun to see what this worried officer would do if she slipped behind the wheel of the VW and started the motor. He was all too clearly concerned that he would be reprimanded if he let her leave. So she went docilely back to the entrance with him and, once inside, got a glimpse of Rick Kettler in an elevator just as the door was closing on him. Having got her inside, the officer on sentry duty left her to herself. The elevator Rick was in was going down. Which meant but one floor. Kim took the stairs and soon stood in the doorway of the room in which she had waited with Emtee Dempsey before going to the studio and the Basil Murphy Show.

Now Lorrie sat at the large round table, all alone, reflected in the mirrors on the wall, her wide eyes dry but filled with wondering fear. Kim stood there half a minute before Lorrie focused and saw her.

"What are you doing here?"

"I came with my brother. He's a policeman. What happened?"

"Basil Murphy is dead."

"Tell me about it." Kim pulled up a chair next to Lorrie. The girl turned her unblinking eyes on Kim. Her lower lip trembled and the tears she had been holding back could be held back no longer.

"They are questioning Rick about it," she blubbered. "They think Rick did it."

One lesson Kim had learned from Emtee Dempsey is the preferability of confronting trouble head on. After comforting Lorrie for a moment, she pushed back from the table and stood.

"Come on. Let's see what's going on."

"They told me to keep out of the way."

Kim made a face. "Where was Basil Murphy found?"

Lorrie got up, wiped her eyes with the back of her hand, and firmed her lower lip. "I'll show you."

From the hallway, past the formidable figure of Officer Gleason who guarded the doorway, Kim caught sight of Rick Kettler being interrogated by several detectives, among them Richard. Kettler turned from one to the other —they seemed to be talking all at once—and the stupefied expression on his face did not suggest the intelligence that enabled him to produce the Basil Murphy Show. It occurred to Kim that the young man would no longer perform this function. Did the police think he would kill his employer and put himself out of work? It was absurd. Lorrie shook her head.

"Mr. Murphy fired him too. When he was interceding for me."

"When was that?"

"Yesterday."

This information introduced the worm of doubt and Kim, who had been about to charge the door and, once inside, tell Richard it was silly to suspect Rick Kettler, settled for quizzing Gleason.

"Has the body been taken away?"

Small eyes studied her from folds of flesh. "You're Lieutenant Moriarity's sister."

"That's right."

Gleason nodded, obviously pleased with his powers of recall.

"The body," Kim reminded him.

He had to think. "Murphy? They bagged him and took him away."

A wave of nausea swept over Kim and she turned to face a woman her own age with a most familiar face—freckled, weatherworn, tanned.

"Are you with the police?" Phonsie Quilmes asked.

"What brings you here, Phonsie?"

"I thought I'd save you—and me—some time. I don't want you to come looking for me."

Kim took the athlete's arm and steered her to the waiting Lorrie. "Sergeant," she said to Lorrie, "I'll be using the room downstairs. Tell Moriarity."

She kept moving with Phonsie, whose preoccupation made her oblivious to the baffled expression on Lorrie's face. Kim got the legendary athlete into the elevator without incident and punched the S button.

"I should have stayed here. Even when I was in the parking lot I told myself it was stupid to run, but I drove halfway to Barrington before I took my own advice. Did the receptionist tell you?"

"I want it all in your own words," Kim said briskly, not liking what she was doing, but imagining how proud Emtee Dempsey at least would be at the way she was exploiting this opportunity. Clearly Phonsie knew something about Murphy's death that she had not yet told the police.

Her story was that she had been contacted by Murphy

and urged to join him in a discussion of Melvin Conroy.

"He writes—wrote—under the name of Geoffrey Chaser."

Kim nodded.

"One of his novels was supposed to be about me."

"*What Do You Lie?*"

"Did you read it?"

"No."

"It doesn't matter. He slandered me and all kinds of people who didn't read it knew that. They had read newspaper accounts or something, maybe heard about it. It was fiction, of course, but his books had a reputation..."

"What did Murphy want to talk about?"

"He wanted all of us to sue the estate of Conroy. Conroy had written a book about Murphy too, I guess. It hasn't appeared yet."

"Sue for damages?"

"I know, I know. When I wanted to sue him, right after that book came out, several lawyers advised me against it. Because I was a public figure. Because it was impossible to prove a fictional character was based on me. Because I would give it even more publicity."

"I suppose you told Murphy that."

"Yes, but I never really believed it myself. I think people ought to pay for what they do." Her face had looked out from the back of Wheaties boxes, there was a scrubbed girlish look about her, and she exuded integrity. "So I told him, sure, I'd come talk with him."

"Hadn't you already talked?"

"Only on the telephone. I told him I would come here. He was crippled, you know."

"Just you and Murphy?"

She frowned. "I thought others were coming."

"What others?"

"Others who had books written about them by Geoffrey Chaser. I'm not sure who, so I won't say. Just because I'm in trouble I don't want to cause trouble for others." She had made commercials for the Girl Scouts. She had made TV spots for the spirit of the Olympics. Phonsie Quilmes obviously lived by the principles she urged on girls.

"I think we can find out who they are."

Phonsie shrugged. "I suppose. The way I figured you could find out I was here."

"The receptionist," Kim said, and Phonsie nodded. Kim felt doubly awful misleading Phonsie, since the woman was so obviously true blue and honest as the day was long.

"And his secretary, or whoever it was, who set it up."

"Tell me about that."

"A woman. Some assistant. Not a secretary. Did he have a secretary?"

"Tell me what happened when you got here."

Phonsie Quilmes had been told where to go when she arrived at WRZR, but she had stopped at the receptionist anyway. Phonsie hesitated. "I think she recognized me. It's a rule I have, always acknowledge recognition. Then I wasn't so sure she did know who I was. She didn't say anything." She said this matter-of-factly, as if she owed such frankness to the world.

Kim said, "You are honest almost to a fault."

Phonsie looked at Kim, her lake blue eyes slightly troubled. Then they were serene again. "I am making up for when I wasn't."

"Oh?"

"In his novel about me he wrote as if I had cheated. I hadn't, not like in the story. But I accidentally grounded my club in a fairway sand trap and that's a violation. It just touched and I didn't call myself on it. I should have. When my playing opponent said I had improved my lie, how my ball was sitting, I denied it. Well, she withdrew the accusation and I didn't disqualify myself, and since that time I have never broken a rule or done anything out of line. That's why the book hurt so. It was like my opponent again, robbing me of the chance of making a clean breast of it. I couldn't admit it then."

"You're admitting it now."

"This is even more serious."

When she doubted that the receptionist recognized her, she followed the instructions she had been given. By Lorrie, Kim would guess. She took the elevator to the studio floor.

"I passed this room and went on down the hall to the studio."

"Why would he want you to meet him there?"

She smiled. "So people would think I was just another guest on his show."

"Go on."

"He wasn't there. No one was there. I waited for a while..."

"Where?"

"In the studio. There was a phone there, so I picked it up and asked to be put through to Basil Murphy. He apologized and told me to come to his office."

"Basil Murphy told you that? What time was it?"

"10:40." She didn't hesitate. "There are clocks all over the studio and for some reason the time stuck in my mind."

"You went to his office?"

"Yes. It must have happened during the time it took me to go from the studio to his office. Just a matter of minutes. Killing someone should take longer, shouldn't it?"

She found Murphy's office and, since it opened onto the hallway and the door was open, she went in after tapping on the frame. Having just spoken with Murphy, she had no hesitation in doing this. He was lying on the floor, inside the door in such a way that those passing by would not have been able to see the body.

"The scarf was still around his throat and his eyes were open." Phonsie kept her eyes on Kim. She paused to swallow. "When I saw that he was dead, I was terrified. My only thought was to get out of there." Her eyes dropped. "And that is what I did."

"But you came back."

"Because I knew my being here would be discovered. That was just more cowardice."

"I don't think anyone else would call it that."

"It was so stupid! What was I afraid of? A dead body? No. My first thought was that I would be blamed."

"Why would anyone think you killed Basil Murphy?"

"If it made sense, I wouldn't have run away. It was an impulse. No. I don't want to pretend I'm not to blame for running. I should have sounded the alarm. What if he was still alive and could have been saved?"

The door was pushed open and Lorrie's frizzled head appeared, but in the wall mirror Kim could see that Richard was with her. She got swiftly to her feet, almost overturning the chair, and when she spoke her voice seemed to come from her throat.

"Lorrie, did you tell Lieutenant Moriarity where we are?"

But her eyes met Richard's in the mirror, and there was no way she could keep the guilt out of hers.

"Sister Kimberly," Emtee Dempsey said, "you acted with great adroitness, and what you have learned is of maximum importance."

"I feel awful, deceiving her like that."

"Nonsense. You let the poor woman unburden herself while she waited to talk with the police."

"She thought I was a police officer."

"Well, after all, you transported Richard there..."

Kim refused to listen. "She is so *honest*, Sister Mary Teresa."

"So you have made clear. With her, honesty is obviously a policy."

"You make that sound disreputable."

"Do I? I shouldn't do that." But there was a lingering note of disapproval in the old nun's voice that Kim could only attribute to her own inability to convey how fresh and frank and wonderful Phonsie Quilmes was. "Well, Richard will get the truth out of her."

"Sister!"

A pudgy little hand waggled in a petition for patience. "I only meant he is unlikely to get anything else. Of course, he will want to pursue the lead she gives him."

"If you talked with her..."

"We must arrange for Messrs. Hawk and Canaris to come talk with us. Basil Murphy will have contacted them too, according to your confidante."

Kim was as close to losing her temper with Sister Mary Teresa as she had ever been. What an impossible old woman she seemed, how perversely intent on seeing something other in Phonsie Quilmes than was there.

"If you want a visitor, I suggest it be Phonsie Quilmes."

"She too, of course, if she cares to come. It would be nice to have them all together."

"All who?"

"All the victims of Melvin Conroy's poison pen. Wasn't that what she told you? That Basil Murphy meant to rally them and lead a charge on the dead Conroy?"

Was that it? That she did not think Murphy capable of attacking Conroy after the author was dead?

Kim excused herself and went to her room, where she sat seething and looking at silvery snow flutter past her window, illumined by the street lamp outside. She had not put on the light in her room. How early dark came, yet how comforting it was in winter, the snow seeming to retain enough daylight to lend a glow to night that never faded. But sitting in a room lit only by light reflected from the snow outside did not give Kim peace.

It was absurd to be so furious with Emtee Dempsey. She was always impossible in one way or another. But this time, Kim thought it was simply wicked of the old nun to continue to suggest that Phonsie Quilmes was anything other than she seemed. Emtee Dempsey was being as unfair as Melvin Conroy! Kim almost wished that thought had occurred to her downstairs. What would Emtee Dempsey have said if Kim had likened her to Geoffrey Chaser?

The thought cheered her up and drove away the rancor. She started when there was a tap at the door, then sat still. If she said nothing, it would be assumed that she had fallen asleep.

"Kim?"

Joyce. Kim turned on the light and opened the door.

"She wants to know if you're still pouting."

Kim flushed with anger, and it didn't help that Joyce was grinning at her. But Joyce stopped her from closing the door.

"Come down and have something to eat. She wants you there when company comes."

"Company?"

"Katherine is coming. And two or three others. She said you'd know who they were."

Seven

In the living room, Sister Mary Teresa sat in a brocade chair facing a fireplace flanked by sofas, on one of which sat two men, on the other Katherine Senski and a Phonsie Quilmes who was clearly very surprised to see Kim. Fortunately, Emtee Dempsey was holding forth on the novels of Philip Canaris and their author was not displeased with the verdict she was passing on them. Aware that she had lost the attention of one of her audience, the old nun turned.

"Ah, Sister Kimberly. I am glad you could join us."

"Sister!" cried Phonsie Quilmes.

"This is Mr. Philip Canaris, the renowned author," Emtee Dempsey said. "The justifiably renowned author."

Canaris had a large nose, a large mustache, and eyes

that bulged. He wore a baggy gray pullover and wrinkled trousers, and when he bowed he seemed to be inspecting the weatherbeaten loafers on his feet.

"Next, Mr. Hawk, at whose restaurant the likes of us cannot afford to eat."

Hawk sputtered a denial through teeth clenched in a smile and bent over the hand Kim had assumed he wished to shake. His hair was parted in the exact center of his narrow head and laid in spiky rows upon it.

"And, of course, you have already met Phonsie Quilmes."

The athlete, hands on her hips, head to one side, dimpled the corners of her mouth, suggesting she would like to be amused. "I thought you were a cop."

"I know."

"You might have told me."

"I can't tell you how sorry I am."

"Nonsense," cried Emtee Dempsey. "If anyone mistook me for a policeman I would certainly want to find out why."

"Well, she certainly found out," the legendary lady golfer said.

"Lieutenant Moriarity is my brother."

"So he told me," Phonsie collapsed back onto the couch she shared with Katherine. "He was madder at you than I was."

"He usually is."

"The good part is that he mentioned Sister Mary Teresa too, so I telephoned and here we all are."

The old nun nodded. "And an extremely good idea it was. All of you have certain interests in common and should share your thoughts. I understand Basil Murphy thought so too. Did he contract you gentlemen?"

"How do you mean?" Hawk asked, leaning forward, anxious to serve.

"Phonsie, why don't you tell us what you told Sister Kimberly?"

Kim was not sure whether hearing the story a second time made her a better or worse appraiser of it. On the one hand, the narrative had a certain practiced air to it, rehearsed, many of the phrases the same ones Phonsie had used when she spoke to Kim in the waiting room at WRZR. Had she spent the time returning to the studio after leaving, going over in her mind what she would say? On the other hand, knowing what would be said, Kim was able to concentrate both on the teller and on the reactions of the two male guests.

Phonsie herself concentrated on Sister Mary Teresa, from time to time turning to look at Katherine Senski beside her, ignoring the men on the facing sofa. Canaris, holding a lighted cigarette between long fingers, his elbow resting on the arm of the sofa, watched Phonsie through narrowed eyes, perhaps to protect them from smoke. Through puckered lips he expelled smoke in a way that suggested a negative reaction to what Phonsie was saying.

Hawk continued to lean forward even from a seated position, but the expression on his face made Kim think he was eavesdropping rather than listening. How often had he been privy to the secrets of the celebrated just because— *pace* Geoffrey Chaser—his discretion could be depended upon?

Neither man responded when Phonsie said she assumed Basil Murphy had contacted them as well.

"Didn't he also mention Madelaine Marr?" Sister Mary Teresa asked.

"No. No, he didn't."

But this summoning of the victims was mere prelude, the reason Phonsie was on the scene at WRZR to find the lifeless body of Basil Murphy.

"Strangled," Emtee Dempsey said.

"There was a scarf around his throat and his face..." Phonsie stopped, closed her eyes, shook her head.

Katherine Senski, who had the wire-service accounts of the murder of Basil Murphy, took them from her purse and read them when asked to do so by her hostess.

"'Basil Murphy, Chicago television personality whose local talk show is syndicated around the country, was found dead in his office at WRZR this afternoon.

"'Preliminary indications were that death was the result of violence, and sources close to the investigation say the victim was strangled.

"'Murphy had recently been the object of attack by Melvin Conroy, who wrote steamy novels under the pseudonym Geoffrey Chaser. Conroy was strangled in his north-side apartment three days ago and Murphy had been questioned by police in connection with the murder.

"'Murphy, a native of Chicago, was educated at...'"

Emtee Dempsey held up a hand and Katherine willingly stopped.

"Both strangled," the old nun said. She nodded at Phonsie. "Go on, my dear."

Canaris said, "Basil Murphy didn't call me."

"You mean he didn't reach you," Emtee said. "You cannot know if he tried to telephone."

"I have an answering service."

Hawk leaned even farther forward. "Nor I. I hadn't heard from Mr. Murphy."

"Perhaps he meant to see you one at a time."

This was a switch. Emtee Dempsey had been systematically skeptical when Kim brought her the athlete's story. Now the old nun seemed determined to make the account gospel truth.

In this version, Phonsie had been tempted to run but had not quite succumbed, leaving the building but, after going to her car in the parking lot and agonizing over what she was doing, deciding to go back inside. No mention of driving halfway home while she was agonizing. During this segment of her story, Phonsie looked directly into Kim's eyes, as if daring her to find a discrepancy. And what if Kim had? Phonsie need only say she had misunderstood the first time.

Kim realized that, if Emtee Dempsey seemed determined to find Phonsie's story plausible, she herself had now adopted the doubter's role. Phonsie had returned to the studio because her vanity had jeopardized her when she went unnecessarily to the reception desk. If her conscience had motivated her, it had been aided by a fear of being remembered by the receptionist—something Phonsie herself had insisted on when she spoke with Kim at WRZR.

"I think more of the idea now than I did while Basil Murphy was still alive," Phonsie said, addressing the two men. "I think we ought to sue Conroy's estate. He slandered us and a judgment in our favor would remove the stain."

Canaris spoke, his words riding an exhaled cloud of

smoke. "I do not consider myself vulnerable to criticism from the likes of Melvin Conroy. Geoffrey Chaser." He pronounced the pen name with contempt.

"Even if he didn't hurt you," Phonsie said, as if stipulating an untruth, "he tried to."

Hawk held up a finger and seemed to be addressing its nail. "Such a case is all but impossible to win. I have consulted my lawyer. First, you must establish that it is indeed yourself on whom the fictional character is based. This can scarcely be done. Even if it could, there is no assurance that a favorable judgment would be made. The result is to bring further bad publicity and nothing else."

"I would not want to get involved," Canaris said, perhaps remembering the embarrassment of those juxtaposed passages in Conroy's comparison of his work and Scott Fitzgerald's.

"How well did you know Conroy, Mr. Canaris?"

"How well? I didn't know him at all."

"You never met?"

"Oh, we met. He introduced himself at a literary banquet sponsored by the *Tribune*." He bowed to Katherine.

"You were never at his apartment?"

"Good God, no."

"Mr. Hawk, did you know Melvin Conroy?"

"He dined at my restaurant on occasion."

"On occasion."

"Regularly."

Kim wondered if the answer would become "often" if Emtee Dempsey persisted. But the old nun had another question. How well did each of her two male guests know Basil Murphy?

"I was once a guest on his show," Hawk said, not without pride.

"I was on it several times, three or four," Canaris drawled. "Nancy Shale was a most persuasive person on the phone. And Basil was always generous in giving me an opportunity to plug a new book. And he was intelligent. Chances were he had actually read the book. This is rare in television interviewers."

"Were you ever on his show, Phonsie?"

She nodded. "Once. Not too long ago." She took a deep breath. "When that book came out. Chaser's. He wanted to give me a chance to answer it, but just being on was a wonderful reassurance. I can't tell you how that novel hurt me. I was sure everyone was talking about me. It was as if I had never won a match. But Basil Murphy was so kind. That appearance changed my whole attitude toward what Conroy had done."

"So you responded when he called on you to come to him."

"Well, as Mr. Canaris pointed out, his wife did the calling."

"Isn't it odd how Melvin Conroy brought you all together?" Sister Mary Teresa smiled at her guests. "But let me offer you refreshments. Sister, will you see if Sister Joyce is busy?"

When Kim pushed into the kitchen the door struck Richard on the forehead and he stumbled backward as Joyce, seated at the table, looked up with rounded eyes and a hand clamped over her mouth.

"What on earth..."

But Richard grabbed her wrists and said in a fierce

whisper. "How did she manage to get those people here?"

"Those people are our guests."

"Well, we've been looking all over for two of them."

"Have you been eavesdropping?"

"I used the entrance Basil Murphy used, that's all. I just got here. Playing a hunch. Where else would Hawk and Canaris be if not here?"

Joyce said, "I offered to tell Sister Mary Teresa he was here."

"Would you like to come in now, Richard?"

"I'll be in the study. Tell Sister Mary Teresa I will wait for her there."

After Richard disappeared up the hallway, Kim told Joyce Emtee Dempsey had offered their guests refreshments.

"I'll help."

"Did you tell him about the envelope?"

Kim stared at Joyce. The envelope containing the paper on which Emtee Dempsey had written the name of the murderer. Kim hurried to the study. Richard was seated in the chair across from the old nun's desk, his head back, his eyes closed. He looked exhausted. He opened his eyes when Kim burst in on him.

"What's wrong?"

"Nothing. Nothing. Would you like a beer or something?"

"A beer would be nice."

"I'll get it."

"Thanks. Thanks, Kim."

But she went by way of the living room where Joyce was taking orders. Kim bent and whispered into Emtee

Dempsey's ear, "Richard is here. He is in the study."

"Ask him to come in." The old nun spoke in her normal voice.

"He wants to talk with you there."

"He should be interviewing my guests."

"I think that's why he came. I'll tell him to come in here."

"No. No, I'll go see him in the study. You help Sister Joyce."

Orders taken, Joyce had gone back to the kitchen. Kim told the guests Sister Mary Teresa would be back in a moment, excused herself, and went to give Joyce a hand. Phonsie wanted beer, Katherine a glass of wine, Canaris Scotch, and Hawk mineral water. No more than five minutes elapsed before Joyce and Kim returned to the living room.

Emtee Dempsey was back in her brocade chair.

There was no sign of Richard.

Kim whispered to Sister Mary Teresa.

"Did you talk with Richard?"

"A glass of wine, dear. Thank you." She refused to meet Kim's eyes.

"A glass of wine," Kim said crisply.

She went into the kitchen, but then immediately down the hall to the study.

It was empty.

To Kim's inquiry when she returned to the living room Emtee Dempsey would only say that Richard had been called away. Had she sent him away? That seemed unlikely. Once inside the house on Walton Street, Richard was difficult to oust. After all, what could they do, call the police? If the old nun had been curious about Richard's coming and going, she had mastered it and was currently absorbed in her conversation with Philip Canaris.

"Abner Singleton?" she said. "But isn't he Melvin Conroy's agent as well?"

A tight little smile from the novelist of deserved renown. "Abner represented me long before Melvin Conroy crawled out from under his rock."

"Conroy was an unusual client for Abner Singleton, was he not?"

"Well, now, Sister, you must never accept a literary agent's claim to being fastidious where the possibility of large amounts of cash are concerned. Abner had principles, but he does not run his agency on altruism. Besides, he took almost illicit pleasure in having the ineffable Geoffrey Chaser in his stable. At first."

"Theirs was a stormy relationship?"

Again Canaris was intent on making the point that writers and agents are in their way natural enemies, necessary evils to one another. "I have had my share of tiffs with Abner, I assure you."

"Did you see Mr. Singleton during his recent visit to Chicago?"

"Oh, he usually managed to squeeze me in when Conroy summoned him to Chicago."

"Why did he come?"

"To kiss and make up with Conroy, if you can believe him, and I remind you he is an agent. To fetch another million-dollar manuscript."

"A novel?"

"*Soi-disant.*"

"What accounted for the reconciliation?"

Canaris smiled, nesting his nose in his now upturned mustache, and rubbed his thumb against the fingertips of his right hand.

"But hadn't Conroy tried to deprive Singleton of his agent's fees?"

"Conroy had no case. Abner knew that. They are bound together with hoops of steel, legally speaking. Abner draws extremely careful contracts. No court in creation would sustain Conroy's exclusion of Abner Singleton from profits made on books for which Abner wrote the contracts."

"But he was legally excluded from later deals?"

"Oh, yes. I don't imagine he ever contested Conroy's right to do that."

"But surely he didn't like it."

"It was Abner's boast, and his shame if it was true, that he had created Geoffrey Chaser from the slime of the earth. My mot was that creation implies change, and Conroy remained slime. Nonetheless, there is truth to the claim that, without the mediation of Singleton—or some other equally shrewd agent—Melvin Conroy would never have achieved the monetary success he did." He looked at his glass. "May I have more of this?"

"Sister Kimberly," Emtee Dempsey began, but Kim had already taken the novelist's glass and started for the kitchen.

"Less water, please," Canaris called after her.

A murmur of television from the basement apartment seemed to explain why Joyce was not in the kitchen. What had Canaris been drinking? Scotch. The medicinal smell of his glass matched that of the Scotch. Kim put three ice cubes and four or five ounces of Scotch in the glass, went to the open door leading to the basement, and saw light under the door below. Why Joyce didn't bring that portable TV up to the kitchen was beyond Kim. But, as with her smoking, Joyce regarded her addiction to television as a series of unconnected episodes. If she were asked about her television habits she would quite sincerely have said she seldom watched it. Kim took the Scotch in to Philip Canaris.

Katherine, noticing this, held up her wine glass. James Oliver Hawk said he might try a taste of the wine, if Sister Kimberly did not mind. Phonsie Quilmes wanted nothing. Kim was aware of the buzz of interesting conversation as she went once more to the kitchen. Is this how Joyce always felt, excluded from the real fun? But pity for Joyce fled when, in the kitchen, Kim picked up again the murmur of the television below.

After she had served the drinks, Kim sat next to Emtee Dempsey and, having waited like a girl about to enter a game of jump rope, said to Philip Canaris, "Did you see Abner Singleton before or after Melvin Conroy was killed?"

The author went on sipping his Scotch, but over the rim of his glass his bulging eyes darted back and forth between Kim and Emtee Dempsey.

"I wondered the same thing," Emtee Dempsey said, as if she thought Canaris might decide Kim's question could be dodged.

He placed his glass carefully on the table beside the couch. "Before," he said. "And after."

"Ah," said Emtee Dempsey, and patted Kim on the arm.

~ 141 ~

"Before *and* after. Before was the usual dull exhortation that I sit down and write *War and Peace*. He is a great nagger, Abner."

"When *can* we expect your next novel?" Sister Mary Teresa asked, and Kim was furious. Who cared how Abner Singleton had urged Canaris on before the murder of Melvin Conroy? The answer was that Emtee Dempsey did. She pursued the topic as if it were the most interesting thing in the world.

"It's always difficult to predict a thing like that," Canaris purred when the old nun asked again when his next novel would appear.

"What is it about?"

"Now there, Sister, you touch upon one of my basic superstitions. Not to talk about work in progress is one of my absolute rules."

"But surely you can give me an inkling of its theme..."

Canaris continued to beam at this interest, but not so brightly as before.

"It has been so long since *Easeful Death*," Emtee Dempsey said.

The smile on Canaris's face faded, his mustache drooped, his glance at Emtee Dempsey was almost accusing.

"A Melvin Conroy may be able to produce novels like sausages, but I confess I cannot."

"But your first three came at two-year intervals, did they not?"

Canaris drank deeply of his Scotch. "They did. Call it beginner's luck."

"I imagine Melvin Conroy's attack must have been difficult to bear. I don't mean that wretched novel, but the piece in the *Tribune* Sunday Magazine displayed a side of him I, for one, would never have suspected."

"What he displayed was me! Or thought he did. He made me out to be little more than a plagiarizer. Can you imagine that toad adopting a moralistic stance with a real novelist?" Canaris's voice rose, Katherine and Hawk stopped talking and stared at him. Aware that he had spoken with emotion, the novelist finished his Scotch. He seemed about to ask for more, then thought better of it.

"That attack has made it very difficult for me to finish another novel. Isn't that why you wanted to know? Well, it's true. My style has always been pastiche, a fictional analogue to the Eliot of *The Waste Land*. The better critics saw that; it was considered my strength, not a weakness. Conroy robbed me of that style ..."

The room fell silent. They had done little mourning of Basil Murphy since these guests had arrived. Now they seemed to be conducting a wake for the demise of Philip Canaris's muse.

"You saw Abner Singleton after the murder of Melvin Conroy?"

Canaris fell upon this change of subject with relief. "Yes. Yes, I had lunch with him and Glen Regensburg. We might have been celebrating."

"Regensburg was his editor?"

"Another link between me and the pornographer. Glen edited all my novels. Like Abner, he made frequent visits to Chicago at the behest of Conroy. I suppose I was the poor beneficiary of his ability to force them to make the journey here. Getting to New York is not what it was, overnight on the Twentieth Century. Now it's up and down on some cheapo flight from Midway."

"Did they come out together?"

"Abner and Glen? Yes. This time, at any rate. They didn't always come at the same time." Canaris considered his empty glass. "In fact, this was the first time they were in Chicago together, at least as far as I know."

"Would you like Sister to freshen your drink?"

"If it's not too much bother."

This time Kim gave him four ice cubes and half as much liquor. It was all well and good for Emtee Dempsey to ply their guests with drink in order to loosen their tongues, but Canaris seemed to have a voracious appetite for Scotch. Luckily, there was not all that much left in the bottle, a gift from Mr. Rush, their lawyer.

She returned in time to hear Canaris remark that the agent and the editor had conferred with Melvin Conroy together.

"Two against one?"

He took his glass without acknowledging the refill; maybe by ignoring the number of his drinks he could keep a firmer grip on sobriety. "Don't worry about Melvin Conroy, Sister. He had people like Abner Singleton and Glen Regensburg for breakfast."

"That early in the day?"

Canaris snorted. "A figure of speech. A rather obscure one, now that I think of it. I meant he was more than match enough for those two."

"Did they confer with Melvin Conroy in his apartment?"

Canaris considered the question. "I don't know."

"Did they speak of Conroy at your luncheon, after he was dead?"

"We spoke of little else. And of course they were happy to have what will now be the posthumous novel. Let's hope the last. You have to grant that man had an ability to attract and hold attention. He was so bad, so awful, so vulgar, he was impossible to ignore."

"Was it the day after the body was found that you had your lunch?"

"I suppose it was. Sounds ghoulish, doesn't it? Three grown men gloating over the death of someone like that?"

"Well, after all, his death did lift pressure from the shoulders of each of you."

"Melvin Conroy exerted no pressure on my shoulders. The pain he caused me was altogether elsewhere, anatomically speaking."

James Oliver Hawk laughed, seeming to surprise himself by doing so, and this brought him and Katherine into the conversation. With the result that it lost any clear focus. The only gain was the information that Canaris, Abner Singleton, and Glen Regensburg had enjoyed their festive lunch at Hawk's restaurant, El Comedor.

"Hawk joined us for a drink. Didn't you, James?"

"You mustn't make that too widely known. Can you imagine my condition if I had a drink with every diner?"

"Of late that would be less demanding, wouldn't it?"

Hawk smiled at Canaris, but spoke to Emtee Dempsey. "Where did you find this wine?"

"It was a gift. Is it good?"

"It is wonderful."

"Our lawyer keeps us supplied with such things. So that we can entertain when the occasion arises. I think he wants to be sure there is something here for himself. Sister, do pour more wine for Katherine and Mr. Hawk."

Kim poured a glass for herself as well, curious to taste the wine James Oliver Hawk found so good. Would he have been surprised to learn it was an Argentinian wine? She sipped it there in the kitchen, a mildly defiant act. A bit petulant, too. She frowned at the basement stairway, wishing Joyce had remained on duty to fetch all these drinks.

"What a scene that must have been," Katherine was saying. "The four of you having a drink together the day after your tormentor was killed."

"I was the only missing suspect," Phonsie Quilmes said, and it was like releasing air from a balloon; the remark seemed to deflate both Hawk and Canaris. "We all are suspects, you know. That's why I wanted us to come here and talk with Sister Mary Teresa. This afternoon's quizzing by the police was not a very pleasant affair."

"My dear lady, they have come to my door too."

"Sure. About Conroy. But will they pester you about Basil Murphy?"

"With as much rhyme or reason as they did you," Canaris said gallantly.

"My lawyer told me I was a fool to talk with them before." James Oliver Hawk looked from face to face. "I do not want to go through that again, with or without a lawyer. They want to know if I had reason to kill Melvin Conroy. Of course I had a reason. We all had reasons."

Katherine said, "Well, one of the benefits of poor Basil Murphy's death should be to divert attention from the three of you. I don't imagine any of you had a reason to kill him?"

Kim thought of Nancy Shales, of Remy Carrero, of the quite different group of people the police would also be interested in questioning about the death of the talk-show host.

"But both men were killed in the same way," Emtee Dempsey said.

Any relief Katherine's remark had brought the trio was gone. Katherine seemed a bit vexed at the suggestion that she had not hit upon a way of exonerating these pleasant people.

"Well, Sister, perhaps now is the time for you to tell us who killed Melvin Conroy."

"I wish you could," Canaris muttered.

"Oh, she can," Katherine said. "She solved it days ago. She wrote the name down and sealed it in an envelope."

Emtee Dempsey burst into laughter and clapped her hands. "Oh, Katherine, you mustn't bother these lovely people with our parlor tricks."

So saying, she put both hands on the head of her cane and boosted herself to her feet. Not the most subtle way to inform guests the evening had come to an end, but effective. Phonsie offered Canaris a ride and Hawk had a car. Katherine lingered after the three had left.

"Don't be mad at me for mentioning your guess, Sister Mary Teresa."

"My guess! Katherine, I did not make a guess. Everything that has happened since I wrote down that name confirms me in thinking I am right. It is a deduction, perhaps, but not a guess."

"Oh, fiddlesticks. I suppose I should be going too."

"Must you?"

"Why on earth not? You all but ordered us from the living room."

"I thought you might want to speak with Madelaine Marr."

"Madelaine Marr?"

"She's downstairs in the guest apartment. With Richard Moriarity and Sister Joyce. Come."

The little nun went through the kitchen to the basement door and Katherine, exchanging a look with Kim, followed.

Eight

Madelaine Marr sat upright in a straight-backed chair, hands folded in her lap, a pietà lacking only her sacrificed son.

The analogy was not, as soon emerged, far-fetched. It was concern for Jorge Higgins that had brought Madelaine to the house on Walton Street. She had intended to talk with Sister Mary Teresa. Finding Richard there seemed an indication of what she was meant to do. She persuaded Emtee Dempsey to return to her guests, she and Joyce and Richard could talk in the kitchen. But of course the basement apartment was better.

Kim saw that the television set was not on. The voices she had heard must have been those of Richard and Madelaine Marr. Had Joyce just sat listening?

"I felt like a chaperone. She would turn to me from

time to time and smile that very sad smile, but basically it was just she and Richard."

Jorge Higgins had fallen off the wagon and, in his cups, confessed to Madelaine Marr that he had killed the infamous Melvin Conroy.

Settling down on a matching straight-backed chair, looking as if she could stay up all night if necessary, Emtee Dempsey said, "And you believed him?"

Madelaine Marr's smile established an intricate pattern of wrinkles on her lean face. If she looked weary in repose, that smile, together with the halo-like effect of the braided hair crowning her head, transformed her. Kim thought, almost with surprise, that Madelaine must have been beautiful once.

"I would not have believed him if he were sober, Sister."

"In vino veritas?"

Madelaine nodded. Richard could not conceal his impatience.

"Sister, I have been telling Miss Marr that more than a claim to have killed Conroy is needed, at least by us." His tone suggested that semi-hysterical women might consider a case closed on the basis of the drunken babbling of Jorge Higgins, but police are made of sterner stuff.

Madelaine reached for the cracked patent-leather purse propped against a leg of her chair and opened it. She drew from it an object wrapped in tissue paper and handed it to Richard.

When he took it, Kim and Joyce leaned forward. Katherine stood and came close as he unwrapped it. An ashtray. A glass ashtray. It bore a legend. The Claremont.

"He gave that to me," Madelaine said. "As proof that he had done it."

"When was that?" Emtee Dempsey said.

"Today. A few hours ago. My first concern was with Jorge. Alcohol works like poison on his system and he needed treatment."

Richard sighed, "Ashtrays like this are scattered around the lobby of the Claremont, they are on every table in the lounge and bar. He wouldn't have to go upstairs to get hold of one of these."

"That's true," Katherine said with some reluctance.

"But he would have to get inside the hotel, Richard," Sister Mary Teresa said. "That in itself is no mean feat, as you described it."

"If he was there, he would have been seen."

"Exactly my point," Emtee Dempsey said sweetly.

Richard glared at her before asking Madelaine Marr, "Where is Higgins now?"

"St. Jude's."

"St. Jude's Hospital?"

"He needs to be detoxified. When Jorge drinks, he knows absolutely no moderation."

"I'll go talk with him." Richard looked at his watch. "In the morning we'll check at the Claremont. Rest easy, Miss Marr. We will disprove his story, I'm sure."

"Did he confess to the murder of Basil Murphy as well?"

"Basil Murphy?"

Clearly Madelaine Marr had not heard of the death of the celebrated television personality. Richard, perhaps wanting to spare Madelaine Marr his witnessing of this further proof of the absurdity of Jorge Higgins's claim, said good-by. Kim went with him to the front door.

Before opening it, he rolled his eyes. "All I can say is, it's easier listening to her than to Emtee Dempsey."

"She's a saint."

"That's what they tell me." He had opened the door and now turned. "You meant Madelaine Marr, didn't you?"

"Her too."

"Bah."

"Can I come with you to the Claremont tomorrow?"

He made a face. "What does she expect you to find that we won't?"

"This is my idea."

He looked at her as if he were going to state his disbelief. But he shrugged. "Be there at 9:30."

He pulled the door closed with a slam and Kim could hear him thump across the porch.

The desire to see the Claremont had been prompted by something Emtee Dempsey had said several days ago, after Conroy's body had been found along with indications that the writer's study had been rifled. The missing diskettes on which Conroy would have stored what he was composing on his word processor had seemed to vindicate Emtee Dempsey's distrust of the computer as a writing instrument. "A typist would keep carbons," she had humphed.

And a writer who used a word processor would keep back-up copies of what he had stored. Kim found it unbelievable that someone who produced the kind of money-making verbiage Conroy did would not take special precautions with his product.

Emtee Dempsey had persuaded her guests to come

upstairs to the kitchen, where Sister Joyce could make cocoa for them. "With marshmallows," she added, gilding the lily.

Joyce was already in the kitchen, putting a pan of milk on the stove.

"Does she realize how late it is?" Kim asked in a whisper.

"Why are you complaining? You had a nap."

The three older women sat around the kitchen table sipping the cocoa Joyce served them and carried on a conversation Kim would not have missed for the world. Representatives of a generation that had been all but universally maligned in the wake of Vatican II, these three women were, each in her distinctive way, heroines of that preconciliar era. More than once Sister Mary Teresa had suggested that the Thirties, Forties, and Fifties would one day be recognized as a golden period in the history of the Catholic Church. Those were the times when laywomen like Madelaine Marr had stirred the souls of many by the heroic life she led, when women like Katherine had shown the way to professional excellence, and when Emtee Dempsey had shown how brilliance can flourish even in the apparently restrictive corridors of the convent.

Anecdote followed anecdote, legendary names were mentioned, and Kim felt drawn back into a better time. When the phone rang, she sprang to her feet and ran down the hall to the study so the three women would not be interrupted.

It was Richard.

"Jorge Higgins took a powder. You better tell Madelaine."

"He's not in the hospital?"

"No one thought he was in good enough shape to go. Not that they were guarding him. He wasn't violent or anything. By the time someone noticed he was missing he could have been gone half an hour."

"Do you suppose he went back to The House?"

"That's where I'm calling from."

"And he's not there."

"Chances are he just hadn't had enough to drink yet. I suppose Madelaine would know where he goes. I know where I'm going. To bed."

"Richard, I don't want to tell her."

"Suit yourself."

But she could not keep the news from Madelaine and, in a pause in the conversation, she said, "That was Richard on the phone."

"More news?" Emtee Dempsey said, as if only another murder could justify this interruption.

"Jorge Higgins left the hospital. When Richard got there he was gone. Apparently he just walked out."

"Oh my God!" Madelaine cried.

"Richard was calling from The House."

"Not there?" Katherine asked.

Kim shook her head.

Madelaine looked at Emtee Dempsey. When she spoke, her voice was low but steady.

"When was Basil Murphy killed?"

Emtee Dempsey had taken out her watch and it popped open when she pressed the stem. "We've done enough talking for tonight. You're both welcome to spend what's left of the night here. There is more than enough room."

"I accept," said Katherine. "I am dead tired."

Madelaine took her purse and stood. "I must get back to The House. Jorge will show up there sooner or later and I have to be there."

"How did you come?"

"The bus."

"Take a cab," Katherine said. "I'll pay for it."

"Nonsense," Emtee Dempsey said. "Sister Kimberly will take you. If you refuse to spend a night in the convent, a nun can spend a night in your establishment."

Kim was at once attracted by the idea and annoyed to have her services volunteered by Emtee Dempsey. She stopped herself from saying she had to meet Richard at the Claremont at 9:30 the following morning. That would have sounded as if she were trying to avoid driving Madelaine back to her legendary refuge for the derelict. And she very much wanted to see The House.

Madelaine directed Kim down a narrow alley flanked by buildings that seemed to resist the perpendicular. Trashcans and debris and shards of broken glass added to Kim's unease. In the passenger seat Madelaine seemed visibly more relaxed than she had on Walton Street, but then, it occurred to Kim, to Madelaine this was home.

Parking the car behind the building that housed The House was like abandoning it. A figure that had been collapsed against a trash can stirred when the VW's headlights illumined the space. A man, apparently drunk; he tried and failed to stay on his feet unaided.

Madelaine got out of the car quickly and went to the derelict, helping him to his feet. Kim stayed in the car with the lights on; it was the only illumination there was. The expertness with which Madelaine got the man balanced against her and started moving him toward the door impressed Kim. Was the man Jorge Higgins?"

A half minute after disappearing inside, Madelaine reappeared. She came and stood beside the car.

"You needn't stay, Sister."

"Of course I'll stay." But only then did she turn off the motor and cut the lights. A strange quiet descended—silence close and in the middle distance, but, far off, the muffled noises of the city. The house on Walton Street was hardly located in a pastoral setting, but Kim had never before felt the presence of the city as she did standing in the dark next to Madelaine Marr behind The House. The silence was less menacing than it was impersonal and indifferent, but perhaps that is the greatest menace of all.

Madelaine put her hand on Kim's arm and led her into the darkened establishment.

The smells—the smell of food, of soup and coffee and other less easily identifiable things as well; the smell of disinfectant, a powerful if subdued olfactory base sustaining all the other smells; the smell of people, of poverty, alcohol, weakness. The smell of breathing. They had entered directly into a dormitory. The shapes of beds became visible and Kim saw that someone was helping the man who had been outside into a bed.

Kim's first impulse was to run, to get out of there, to go back to the house on Walton Street where she belonged. Madelaine's hand was still light on her arm. She knew this saintly woman would not object if belatedly she took her suggestion that she go home. But light as it was, that hand on her arm restrained her. Not forcibly. In the kitchen on Walton Street, listening to Madelaine recall the origins of her work among the derelict, Kim's pulse had quickened at the heroism. How easy from a distance to romanticize that effort, imagining the poor as mere opportunities for heroic action. But here in this odorous place Kim felt no attraction whatsoever to the work that had claimed most of Madelaine Marr's adult life.

Behind the kitchen was a room with four beds, three night tables, and a ceiling light that suffused the scene with insufficient wattage. Kim was given one of the beds, having been introduced to the occupant of one of the others, a very large woman named Grace, who nodded bleary-eyed and burrowed her gray head back into the pillow. Another of the beds was occupied too, a blanket pulled almost completely over a head of golden hair. Madelaine's room opened off this common one and Kim got a glimpse of it before they said good night.

It looked like a cell.

A bed, a small throw rug beside it, a floor lamp drawn up next to it, a three-shelf bookcase not six feet wide whose contents were pushed in every which way, and over the bed a fairly gaudy unframed picture of the Sacred Heart.

"I go to six o'clock Mass if you want to come."

"Wake me," Kim said bravely. It was now after two.

Years ago, when she had entered the novitiate, Kim had spent the first night sleepless, listening to the unintelligible sounds of the convent, heat pipes banging, a ghostly creaking of floors, the sound of the wind trying the corners of the building, achieving gale-level decibels as it did so.

On the ceiling, light flickered. It was where Kim had wanted to be, but now that she was there she could not sleep. And strange as it was, incredible as was the realization that here she was, Kim Moriarity, actually in the convent, she had felt at home.

Not everyone who entered the novitiate stayed. Lying sleepless in Madelaine Marr's establishment, Kim wondered if this is how those without vocations had felt. One girl had not lasted two days. If she had felt as Kim did now, it had been high heroism to remain so long.

Kim was asleep when Madelaine wakened her at 5:30. She washed in silence in tepid water, and in the cloudy mirror over the sink could see Madelaine in her room, seated on the bed, eyes closed. Praying?

Through gray streets to an ugly church of smoky stone crammed between two later no less ugly buildings on its narrow lot. Inside, a veritable fire hazard of vigil lights, figures huddled among the pews, the morning light having forced its way down the narrow space left by the neighboring buildings gave a suggestion of color to the windows. Kneeling beside Madelaine, Kim tried to pray, to concentrate, to dedicate her day to God. Nine-thirty loomed in her mind like a reprieve; she had a genuine excuse to get away from The House. Could she leave in time to swing by Walton Street for a shower?

A bell rang and a bent-over priest emerged from the sacristy in a bass fiddle chasuble of a kind Kim had not seen in years. It was a fast Mass, though devoutly said, and Kim thought, this liturgically retrograde service is the basis of Madelaine Marr's life.

"Did we wake you last night?" Madelaine asked when they were walking back to The House.

Kim looked puzzled. If asked, she would have said she had not slept a wink in the narrow bed with its boardlike sheets.

"Jorge came back," Madelaine explained.

"How is he?"

"Dead to the world." She winced. "He is lucky he isn't really dead to the world."

"You don't really think he killed anyone, do you?"

Madelaine looked straight ahead. Walking, she leaned forward, as if defying prevailing winds, and her profile seemed the weatherbeaten one of a peasant woman. "If what he said was fantasy, I want someone else to show it was."

They ate in the refectory with Madelaine's clients, a room filled with trestle tables covered with oil cloth. Coffee in thick mugs, toast no longer very warm, and oatmeal, all the oatmeal one could want. In Kim's case that was half a bowl. She tried not to stare at the occupants of the other tables. Bleak-faced men with vacant, washed-out eyes, stubbled faces with downturned mouths. Yet they ate with relish. Sun spilled into the room through high bright windows and lay like hope upon the derelicts.

"Is Jorge here?"

Madelaine shook her head. "The doctor gave him something."

"Will he go back to the hospital?"

"That was a mistake. I should have kept him here."

What was the nature of Madelaine Marr's attachment to Jorge Higgins? That he regarded her as a living saint seemed clear enough. The fact that she gave credence to his claim to have killed her tormentor, and his, indicated she shared the general view that he would do anything for her. But her attitude toward Jorge seemed to be more than that she had toward all the other men who came to her for help, even those few who, like Jorge, stayed on to help her. Not that Kim imagined an ongoing romance. Better to put it in the same class as Katherine Senski's doomed love.

It was nearly nine when Kim left. She drove carefully out the alley and into the street and did not floor the gas pedal as she, to her own disgust, wanted to.

Jorge had been in the bar of the Claremont at least, having sailed past the sentries and into the dimly lit room where expensive people sipped overpriced drinks and looked up alarmed at the entry of this reminder of another grimier world outside.

Richard talked with Sidney the bartender upstairs in the apartment of the late Melvin Conroy. Sidney's mass of mahogany hair looked odd in back and Kim realized it was not real. The handlebar mustache, on the other hand, was. Large designer glasses seemed to complete the effort to conceal his real self.

"I told you all I know," Sidney groaned. "I never saw a guy in a wheelchair. I never saw a masked man in a cape neither." He grinned at Kim, inviting complicity.

"You didn't tell us about the drunk who nearly broke up your bar the night Conroy was killed."

"Broke up the bar? Come on. He wasn't there five minutes."

He wouldn't have been there that long if he had not seized an ashtray and dared the doormen and bartender to eject him. Jorge was already very drunk. Sidney had paid no attention to what the guy was babbling, just keeping his attention while Raoul crept on hands and knees along the wall and then leaped up and pinned the drunk's arm.

"We gave him the heave-ho and that was it. I should mention that when you want a murderer?"

Where Melvin Conroy worked was meant to be a dining room. He had turned it into a study dominated by a wall of computer equipment. An IBM PC, a laser printer, a monitor with cinnamon letters.

"You know what you're doing?" Richard asked.

Kim sat at the desk and put her fingers on the keyboard of Conroy's computer. A hard disk. She pulled up its index. Blank. There was a glass-covered tray for storing diskettes on the desk. His back-ups? Kim lifted the glass lid and ran her fingers over the tops of the labeled dividers, recognizing the titles of the infamous novels. Places for diskettes, but no diskettes. The final label was unfamiliar.

Richard let Sidney go and the little bartender strutted in his Cuban-heeled loafers to the door. His maroon jacket and bow tie seemed badges of office, or medals earned for providing enervating drinks in the semidark to those for whom the world was momentarily too much. Richard stood beside Kim's chair.

Kim said, "Someone really cleaned him out. The hard disk erased, all his back-ups gone."

"Yeah."

It seemed a metaphor of death, an absence, a slate wiped clean, only a lingering trace that a human person had sat here by the hour hitting that keyboard.

"I wonder who wanted it all?" Kim asked.

"The murderer."

"But who's that?"

"Ask Sister Mary Teresa. Didn't she write it down and seal it away when you were playing games?"

Kim thought of that on the way back to Walton Street. That the old nun had made a guess was clear enough, but she had made it at a time when she had not known what she now knew and had not met so many of those involved. Would she want to change her mind now?

Nine

Nancy Shale was with Sister Mary Teresa in the study. She looked up at Kim, a long-fingered hand holding a florid scarf to her throat.

"My cold's better."

"Which is my good luck," Emtee Dempsey said. "I had been wanting to have this conversation with you ever since Sister reported on her visit to your apartment."

"Did you tell her everything?" Nancy Shale looked at Kim half saucily, half warily.

"If you mean, did Sister mention your paramour, the answer of course is yes. It would have been a very incomplete report if she had not included his dramatic entry."

"And exit," Kim said. "I am sorry about your husband's death."

The large eyes widened further and the full-lipped

mouth fell open. But when she spoke, it was in a small voice. "Thank you."

"Have you made funeral arrangements yet?" Sister Mary Teresa asked.

"No!" She looked back and forth from Emtee Dempsey to Kim. "What kind of hypocrite do you think I am? Remy Carrero is taking care of everything." She sat back and inhaled deeply, her eyes closed. "I have broken up with Pablo."

"Good," Kim said, then wondered who had done the breaking up.

Emtee Dempsey said to Kim, "And what did you learn at the Claremont?"

"Richard spoke again to the bartender who was on duty the night of the murder. I checked the computer."

"And?"

"The bartender remembered Jorge. He had put on a scene and been thrown out. It was while resisting ejection that he picked up the ashtray and threatened people with it. He's lucky they simply let him go."

"That will be a relief to Madelaine. But what of the computer?"

"Nothing is stored on its hard disk and all the diskettes on which he made back-ups are gone. There was a place for the new one. He labeled it work in progress, then crossed that out and gave it a title."

"That must be the manuscript his agent and editor were so happy to get. I wonder from whom? What had he named it?"

Kim glanced at Nancy Shale before answering. *"Wheelie."*

The old nun nodded. The title seemed to make it inescapable that this was the threatened novel about Basil Murphy. Nancy Shale rose and looked at the two nuns.

"I wish this had been under happier circumstances. Nonetheless, I have enjoyed our visit, Sister Mary Teresa."

Nancy Shale, if she had drawn the same conclusion from the title of Conroy's last novel, did not say so. Kim saw her to the door and came back to a brooding Emtee Dempsey. Blue eyes stared sightlessly at an opposite wall of books.

Kim said, "If there were only Melvin Conroy, I would think she had done it."

The old nun looked at Kim. "What did you say that bartender's name was?"

"I don't know that I did."

"Please call and ask him to come to see me."

"What reason could I give?"

The old nun thought a moment. "Ask if he ever works for private parties."

The small bald man who stood on the porch when Kim opened the door might have been a stranger, except for the handlebar mustache.

"Sidney?"

"You? I thought this was about a party."

"Please come in. You've come to the right place."

If Kim had expected to sit in on the conversation with the bartender, she was disappointed. Emtee Dempsey dismissed her after a slightly terrified Sidney, unable not to stare at the little old nun in the incredible habit, sank into the chair offered him. "Thank you, Sister," Emtee Dempsey said.

There were times when Kim would have been delighted to be absent from sessions in the study, but on this occasion she was consumed with curiosity. Why on earth had Emtee Dempsey wanted to talk to Sidney? She had not pressed her on it before the man's arrival, since she had assumed she would find out in good time. Now, having pulled the door of the study closed, she stood for a moment glaring at it.

"Kick it." Joyce spoke in a stage whisper from the kitchen door.

Kim went down the hall and into the kitchen, where she poured herself a cup of coffee. If she kept busy, if she had some coffee, she would be better able to control her anger.

"Who's the guest?"

"A bartender."

"Come on."

"I mean it. From the Claremont. He was on duty the night Melvin Conroy was killed. He's the one who told Richard about Jorge."

"What does she want with him?"

"I don't know."

"Well," Joyce said after a moment, "if it's a secret..."

"Joyce, I really don't know. She didn't tell me. And she didn't want me to stay in the study."

"Hmmm."

Kim might have gone up to her room and taken a nap. She might have gone into the chapel to regain her composure and say some prayers. She might have gone for a walk

on this glorious day when sun spilled onto the accumu-
lated snow, giving almost the illusion of spring. What she
did was stay right there in the kitchen, drink three cups of
coffee, and wait for Sidney's visit to end. Any fair observer
could see she had mastered her pique and was prepared to
answer a summons from the study.

"She shouldn't be alone with a man," Joyce said. "Behind closed doors."

"Tell her."

"I'd rather tell the bartender."

Sidney was with Sister Mary Teresa nearly forty-five
minutes before the study door opened and he came swiftly
down the hall to the front door. His expression gave no
clue to what had transpired. Kim hesitated before letting
him out.

"She wasn't all that terrifying, was she?"

He looked at her vaguely. Then his eyes focused.
"She's really something."

"We think so. Have a good talk?"

"Sister Kimberly, could you come here." Emtee
Dempsey stood in the hall outside the study, leaning on
her cane. Kim pulled open the door and Sidney darted outside.

"What did you find out?" Kim asked when she joined
the old nun.

"That I have been right all along."

"Sidney assured you of that?"

"Let me say simply that he provided an important fact
that sustains my earlier inference."

"Which is?"

Emtee Dempsey steepled her pudgy fingers, elbows

on the arms of her chair. Thus she had used to lecture her classes.

"The murderer was in the bar of the Claremont that night. That solves the mystery of entrance. The murderer was already in the hotel."

"And Sidney knows who it is?"

The lenses of her glasses sparked briefly when she turned. "Oh, the man has no idea at all of the implications of what he told me."

"Who was in the bar that night, Sister?"

Emtee Dempsey hesitated, but if she felt any impulse to vindicate her claim to have seen long since who Conroy's murderer was, she conquered it.

"Later, Sister Kimberly."

Not sufficient audience for the great revelation? Kim was still on a low boil from having been excluded from the conversation with Sidney, but this further insult raised her temperature again.

"Would you like me to phone Richard so you can tell him his work has been done for him?"

"Irony, Sister? Now, now. In any case, that is not the message I would wish you to give Richard. He has much left to do. I would like to see him, though."

He was not in his office, so Kim left a message that had still not been answered when they were preparing to retire. Emtee Dempsey asked about it as Kim was helping her down the hallway to the chapel for night prayers.

"No. Not unless Joyce took a call."

But Joyce had not received Richard's answer to Emtee Dempsey's request that he call.

* * *

The news came the following morning, when they were at table, by radio and by newspaper. Joyce had WBBM on in the kitchen and it was quite audible in the dining room, where Emtee Dempsey had the *Tribune* propped before her as she ate. She was a longtime fan of John Madigan and would stop reading the paper when the veteran reporter's oral essay aired just before the hour. But it was a regular news item on the radio that combined with the story on page three to bring an uncharacteristic gasp from the old nun.

"Dear God!" She looked across the table at Kim.

"I didn't hear it. What is it?"

But Sister Mary Teresa sat stunned, her expression one of deep remorse. "It is unforgivable that I did not foresee the danger. I brought it about, Sister. I precipitated it. Call Richard and insist on being put through to him. Perhaps if he had answered my call...No. I will not try to put the blame for this on him."

"Would you please tell me what has happened?"

The newspaper was handed across to Kim. Nothing leaped out at her. There was a photograph of a cabbie who had just won several million in the state lottery and seemed to be suffering from the confusion of those whose wilder prayers are answered. The story occupied the two right-hand columns of the page under the headline Chicagoan Garroted by Intruder. The name was not give until the second paragraph.

Hirschell. Sidney Hirschell.

Emtee Dempsey had pushed away from the table. She crossed the room to the telephone but, having picked it up, just stared at it. Kim got up to make the call for her.

Richard was not in. Yes, the message had been left for him. No, it was not known when Lieutenant Moriarity would be in. Yes, the message would be put once more on his desk.

"Can't you contact him in some way?"

"Who did you say you were?"

"I am his sister."

"Family business? I'm afraid you'll have to wait for him to call. We don't use police communications for personal matters."

The line went dead. Emtee Dempsey had depressed the cradle.

"He is dodging me, Sister Kimberly."

"I'll call his home."

"No. We have a job to do. It falls on my shoulders now and it is only fitting that I do it alone. Finish your breakfast and then we will be going out."

"Where?"

"Eat."

Kim also read the enigmatic account of the strangling of Sidney Hirschell. He lived on the south side; the speculation was that he had surprised a burglar. The apartment was fairly torn up, but there was no sign of forced entry. Had the assailant been an acquaintance? The investigation continued. The story did not say where Sidney worked.

"What's up?" Joyce asked, joining Kim at the table for a cup of coffee. Emtee Dempsey had gone off to prepare for their errand.

"She wants to go out. Did you hear about Sidney?"

"Who's Sidney?"

"The man who was here yesterday. The bartender from the Claremont."

Joyce ran a finger along the lines of type. "Wow! Isn't that weird. The poor little guy."

Kim had a sudden vision of Sidney's enormous toupee, bereft of its owner, lying with his other belongings in the torn-up apartment where he had lived. An irreverent thought occurred. It should be hung in the bar of the Claremont, like a cardinal's hat in his cathedral, a memorial.

"She wants to go over there?"

"Apparently."

But in the car, Emtee Dempsey shook away the suggestion. "Of course not. We are going to see Nancy Shale."

"Nancy Shale!"

A grim little nod. "Before she does any further harm."

She received them in a jogging costume, sweatband around her head, still keyed up from her morning run.

"I was just about to take a shower."

"Nancy, we must talk."

Nancy tucked in her chin and lifted her brow. "Talk? Of course we can talk. Care for juice?"

"We have already breakfasted."

"Well, I haven't."

"Go ahead."

On her way to the kitchen, Nancy stopped and threw a look at the old nun. "That almost sounds like offering me a final meal."

"Sidney Hirschell is dead, Nancy."

~ 171 ~

"I heard it on the news. I wear a Walkman when I run."

"He was killed."

"I said I heard it."

Emtee Dempsey had followed Nancy Shale into the kitchen and now tried unsuccessfully to get onto a stool at the breakfast bar. Kim decided against helping her up.

"Killed in the same way Melvin Conroy and your husband were killed."

Nancy had put something into the blender and now flicked a switch. There was a roar while the machine reduced its contents to homogeneous gruel. Then silence, and Nancy pouring the result into a glass. She turned and faced Sister Mary Teresa.

Doing what she had been told, Kim stood in the kitchen door. There was no other exit from the rear of the apartment. Shouldn't the law require an alternative? But what law could protect anyone on this twenty-fourth floor if fire broke out below?

Sister Mary Teresa said, "You and I know the connection between those three murders, Nancy. I have come here to make sure there are no more."

"Like who?"

"Have you made arrangements to go to New York?"

"New York?" Nancy laughed and looked at Kim. She drained the contents of her glass.

"Abner Singleton and Glen Regensburg have returned to New York. With the manuscript of *Wheelie*."

"Not a very catchy title."

"I believe the analogy is with groupie. You know the word? You know its implications?"

"Tell me."

"When did you find out that Melvin Conroy's new novel was to be an attack on you, not Basil Murphy?"

"Have you seen it?"

"Did you destroy the diskettes or hide them somewhere? It doesn't matter. A printed copy exists."

"You don't know that."

"The important thing is that you are convinced of it. It was I who inadvertently gave you cause to think so. Just as it was I who unforgivably roused your fear of Sidney Hirschell. You had to assume he would remember your being in the bar that night if questioned further, just as the mention of Jorge Higgins had come up later. You could not take the risk."

Nancy Shale seemed to have become aware that Kim was in effect blocking the exit from the kitchen. Kim shifted, occupying the very center of the doorway.

"Were you alone, Nancy?"

Suddenly arms closed around Kim from behind and she was forced forward into the kitchen until she was shoved painfully against the breakfast bar.

"No," a voice said, speaking past Kim's ear. "Not alone. I was with Nancy."

Kim twisted to see the leering face of Pablo Quince. He dipped toward her and she lurched away, but nonetheless his taunting kiss grazed her cheek.

"I thought as much," Emtee Dempsey said, unruffled. She kept her eyes on Nancy Shale, ignoring Pablo Quince. "You could scarcely afford to let him run free now, could you? How much does he know?"

Nancy Shale smiled. "You do have guts. Or don't you realize the tables have just been turned?"

"To what purpose?"

~ 173 ~

"I'm trying to decide."

"Is it the order of precedence that poses problems? Surely I must be taken care of before Pablo."

"Don't forget your inquisitive companion."

"Sister Kimberly? I am quite conscious of the fact that I have led her into danger. I am sure she is equally conscious of our plight. But is your young man?" Emtee Dempsey did turn now. "Young man, let go of Sister Kimberly!"

Pablo's response was to make another try at kissing Kim. Kim brought her heel swiftly back into his shin and there was a satisfying yelp of pain as she broke free. Pablo hopped back to the doorway.

"Are you aware of the danger you face?" Kim demanded of Pablo.

"What the hell is she talking about?" the degenerate star asked Nancy Shale.

"I am talking of the fact that you have been cohabiting with a murderess," Emtee Dempsey said. "What knowledge do you have of what she has done?"

"Leave him alone!" Nancy Shale cried. She had snatched a towel from a rack and, holding it by two corners, began to twirl it.

"Ah, your weapon. You have what the police would call an MO. A modus operandi."

Nancy came around the breakfast bar, her eyes locked with Emtee Dempsey's. Doubtless that was why she did not see that the old nun had put out her foot. Tripping over it, Nancy lost her balance and Emtee Dempsey turned and gave the woman a great shove. This sent her stumbling toward Pablo in the doorway. He put up his hands, but her momentum carried them into the dining room. Kim swung

~ 174 ~

the door shut on them. The relief that flooded through her evaporated when she found the door had no key.

Emtee Dempsey had taken down the wall phone. "What is the emergency number?"

"911."

A crisp description of impending mass murder was given by the old nun. She put up the phone and joined Kim at the closed door.

Kim said, "Do you think they'll run?"

A shake of the head. "She'll be back." She looked around the kitchen, then took the heavy glass jar from the blender and handed it to Kim. "You stand there." She indicated a place beside the door. "Use that to stun, not to kill."

She took up her position where she would be the first thing seen when the door was opened. Kim, with her glass weapon, would be out of sight beside the door. Kim thought of Jorge Higgins and his ashtray.

The doorknob began to turn slowly. A full revolution, and then it stopped. There was a hand holding the latch open from the other side of the door. Suddenly the door flew open and Pablo Quince, shoulder lowered, hurtled across the kitchen. Emtee Dempsey stepped aside, a chubby matador, and the rock star crashed into the wall. Kim waited, but Nancy Shale did not follow.

"Where is Nancy?" Emtee Dempsey asked the bewildered Pablo.

"Taking a shower."

"Ah. You are wondering about what I said."

"What were you talking about?"

Emtee Dempsey studied the man's face. "I believe you don't know, young man. Very well. Stay here with us until the police come."

"Police?"

And then they arrived. Kim let them in and Emtee Dempsey greeted the three officers, two male and one female, who came into the apartment, looking searchingly around, and then, in a second take, back at Emtee Dempsey. It had occurred to them that an elderly nun in the full flamboyant habit of the Order of Martha and Mary was an unusual person to bring them on the run.

She assured them she had called. "The person responsible for three murders is in the bathroom. Sister Kimberly, take this officer to Nancy Shale."

Officer Kadar had the rolling gait of a sailor. She had taken out her gun and held it at the ready as they went through Nancy Shale's bedroom. From the bathroom came the sound of running water, the shower. The jogging outfit lay scattered across the floor of the bedroom, trailing toward the bedroom.

Officer Kadar tried the door. Locked. She rapped on it forcefully and listened. Only the sound of running water. She looked at Kim.

"Who is she?"

"Nancy Shale."

The name meant nothing. "She really kill somebody?"

There were any number of possible answers to that. At the least, she might have said Emtee Dempsey thought so. "Yes," she answered. "She killed three people."

Kadar stepped back, lifting her foot, and gave one decisive kick at the door, her heavy shoe hitting the knob. The door bent but did not give. The second kick did it. The door swung jerkily into the steam-filled room.

Nancy Shale was slumped in the bathtub with the

stinging ray of the showerhead pelting her. The tub was half full. Her arms were limp at her sides. From her wrists wisps of blood flowed, wreathing the roiled water with arabesques of red.

Ten

Lorrie and Rick Kettler came by with two items of good news: WRZR was taking a chance on Rick to continue the Basil Murphy Show, appropriately renamed, and they were getting married.

"Wonderful," Emtee Dempsey said. "Thank God some good has come out of this sad sequence of events."

Nancy Shale's suicide attempt had failed, she would eventually stand trial for the murders of Conroy, Basil Murphy, and poor little Sidney. "And all that to prevent a novel from being published." The old nun shook her head. "Conscience is a mysterious thing."

In *Wheelie*, a character very much like Nancy Shale is responsible for the mysterious death of her first husband, whose boat is found drifting unmanned in Lake Michigan.

Just so had Nancy Shale's first husband disappeared. Conroy's troubled heroine—Frances Slate—goes on to marry a handicapped TV news announcer whom she manipulates in exaggerated fashion. But it was the implication that she had been responsible for the death of her first husband that had determined Nancy to destroy the book and its author.

"But Basil Murphy?"

"He wasn't in Conroy's apartment," Rick Kettler said, "but was determined to get hold of that novel, which he thought attacked him. I went for him and made copies of Conroy's diskettes."

"How on earth did you get inside?"

"I telephoned the hotel, said I was Conroy, and that a computer repairman would be coming to the hotel to check the computer. The manager or his designer was to be in the room with me at all times."

"And they admitted you on the basis of a phone call."

Kettler nodded his approval. Lorrie, beside him, began to nod in unison with her beloved. "I gave a number and told them to check it after I hung up."

"What number did you give them?"

"Mine."

Rick Kettler said, "Speaking as Conroy, I said I could be reached at the apartment of a friend. It must have been his reputation as a womanizer that explained why that worked. Lorrie played the girlfriend."

The famous blush suffused her cheeks. She groped for Rick's hand and held it as he told of making copies of the diskettes containing the new novel.

"Of course I thought I was protecting Basil Murphy. I

~ 179 ~

printed out a copy and he was furious. The novel attacked his wife."

Kim listened to this exchange, and to another with Richard, in which he tried unsuccessfully to suggest that Sister Mary Teresa had acted unwisely in confronting Nancy Shale with her suspicions.

"Not so, Richard, and you know it. I tried to reach you, many times, as you can easily verify. My worry was that any delay might endanger others."

"Others?"

"Abner Singleton and Conroy's editor, who had a copy of the novel in their possession."

"Where did they get it?"

"You don't doubt they have it, I hope."

"I asked who gave it to them."

"At this point, not a very interesting question."

But Lorrie had told them that Rick had turned it over to Singleton. By that time, he too had come to suspect Nancy Shale.

Richard said, "I suppose that is how the mark of Murphy's wheelchair got onto Conroy's rug."

Emtee Dempsey said nothing, and it was a triumph of politeness over her usual straightforward way of dealing with Richard. The mark of the wheel had been on a throw rug, not the wall-to-wall carpet. The rug belonged in Basil Murphy's office. Rick Kettler and Lorrie were shocked when Emtee Dempsey asked if they had put it there.

"Nancy Shale," Emtee Dempsey had murmured.

It was Katherine, of course, who reminded Emtee Dempsey of the sealed envelope containing the name of the murderer. The old nun was reluctant to take it out and held it in both hands, her eyes down.

"I was wrong, Katherine, and I admit it. The basis for my inference was faulty and I must take responsibility for that."

Katherine, about to crow in triumph, was overcome with sympathy for her old friend.

"No, Sister, the fault is mine. I taunted you and forced your hand. If you made an error, I must share the responsibility."

Kim and Joyce exchanged a look. This subdued and humbled Emtee Dempsey was an unusual sight.

"Who was your guess?" Joyce asked.

Emtee Dempsey winced as if from a blow. "Very well. Call it a guess. I insisted it was an inference and so it was, but the premise was false."

Katherine stood and got hold of the sealed envelope. In her seat, she held it against her forehead and closed her eyes. "Should I guess whose name is written here?"

"Open it, Katherine," Kim said. She did not want Emtee Dempsey's discomfort prolonged. The quicker they learned who she had mistakenly thought was the murderer, the sooner they could switch the conversation in a more comfortable direction.

Katherine tore open the envelope, extracted the piece of paper, and unfolded it. She squinted as she read, looked almost angrily at Emtee Dempsey, then returned to the paper.

Kim and Joyce crossed the room to see what was written on the sheet of paper. Katherine held it to the light. In the bold handwriting of Sister Mary Teresa was unmistakably written Nancy Shale.

"You were right!" Kim cried. Why was she so relieved?

"You got it," Joyce said, equally elated.

"Why have you toyed with us?" Katherine demanded. "You had it right all along and pretended to have made a mistake."

Pudgy hands went up in dismay. "Because my reason was wrong. When I wrote that name, I suspected her because it would have been a way to protect Basil Murphy. Later, when I suspected her real motivation, remembering what Basil Murphy had told me in this very room, I wanted to destroy this envelope. To point to the right person for the wrong reason is no cause for pride. No, I have failed."

"If you insist," Katherine said. "Your inference may have been wrong but your intuition was correct."

"Intuition!" cried the old nun, "Intuition!"

While her little lecture on reasoning and logic got under way, Katherine sat back in her chair with a rustling sound, Kim propped up her chin with her hand, and Joyce went to the kitchen to fetch refreshments.

VOID

VOID

MOREAU SEMINARY LIBRARY
NOTRE DAME, INDIANA 46556